BETWEEN TWO WORLDS

BRIAN SMITH

Prologue

While the nation celebrated its first Thanksgiving since the war's end, Tony drove his pick-up truck from Los Angeles to Manzanar with his wife, their six-month-old son, and his brother. They came to claim Mr. Fukuoka's remains. There was no one else. Mrs. Fukuoka had been in poor health for some time, and their only child had died years earlier.

The Piccinins slept outside the gates with the others—Amy and the baby in the cab, and Tony and Marco on the truck's bed. In the morning, the procession of battered vehicles wound its way through the prison grounds to the makeshift cemetery in the back. Locating Mr. Fukuoka's wooden marker, Tony and his brother used pickaxes and shovels to recover the casket. They stayed, helping the Japanese to exhume their loved ones.

Later, the scavengers and fortune hunters were allowed in. They took doors, furniture, windows, and anything of value, before loading their treasures and heading out.

The only road outside Manzanar was clogged with people trying to sell their newfound treasures. With passage impossible, Tony pulled over. They ate, and Amy nursed the baby. Exhausted, they napped while Tony watched as the bulldozers plowed the buildings, guard towers, and other structures into huge mounds of rubble. After the crowd dispersed, Tony started the long drive to Fresno and Mrs. Fukuoka. As dusk fell, the horizon in his rearview mirror turned reddish-orange from the piles of wood burning at Manzanar.

* * * * *

1

Years later, Tony and Amy took a family trip to Yosemite National Park. They used the park's eastern exit and pulled onto Highway 395 South. The road was now paved. They stopped at Manzanar. Except for the front gates and an occasional concrete slab, everything was gone. As Tony explained to their four children what had happened here, he noticed the tears streaming down his wife's face. At that moment, he vowed that his great, great-grandchildren would know the truth about the concentration camp.

Chapter One

Tony started the twenty-first morning of October 1941 by delivering the *Los Angeles Times* from a satchel slung low over one shoulder. His battered sneakers pumped the pedals of the Monark bicycle he had received as a Christmas present years ago, and a garnet windbreaker with a tear in one sleeve, protected him from the cool air. Tony had eighty-seven customers, and he knew them all—where they were from, how badly their homes needed painting, which couples argued, and most importantly, how promptly they paid him.

At five eleven, Tony was all muscle and no longer the scrawny kid who had to reload his bag at the mid-point. His days of being called half-pint by the older boys in the neighborhood were long behind him.

He tossed the folded newspapers onto door stoop after door stoop. With only a half-dozen or so houses left, his bag now sagged weightless. This was his favorite part of the day. Work was almost finished, and the sun was rising over the San Gabriel Mountains.

Around the bend, he heard the LaRue boys arguing the way they did most morning. Playing catch, the older boy would be neatly groomed—his brother, hair hanging in his eyes and shirttail out. Tony rounded the curve and threw a newspaper to Gino, the younger of the two, who caught it, but he did not show off like usual.

"What's wrong?" Tony asked, knowing something was amiss.

"Stupid tossed the ball too high," Gino said, pointing at Peter. "Now it's stuck."

Peter stood under the tree, looking up, but he was too short to reach the first branch and hoist himself up. Tony jumped off his bicycle and scaled the sycamore with the ease of an orangutan. "That's

3

a freak throw if I've ever seen one," he said, dropping the wayward baseball down.

"Thanks, Tony," Gino said, pushing his hair out of his face. "I'll be there on Thursday. You pitching?"

"Yeah," Tony said, jumping out of the tree. As the LaRue boys returned to playing catch, Tony wished he was eleven again, the perfect age.

He threw a few more papers before swooping into the driveway of a home at the end of Pleasant Oak. A widow in her late seventies spied his approach through the bay window and stepped outside, as she did most days. She was lonely and enjoyed talking to anyone. She held a baker's box; tied with kite string in one hand, and her other hand clutched her burgundy housecoat against her throat. Tony dismounted and jogged up the walk to deliver the paper to her. He was always tempted to just toss it to her, but he knew there would be hell to pay if his parents found out. "Happy Birthday, Tony! I made cupcakes," she exclaimed, handing him the box.

"Thank you, Mrs. Morga," Tony replied.

"Is this your last day?" she asked.

"Yeah, at three-fifteen this afternoon, I officially turn eighteen and Marco takes over," he grinned.

She laughed. "When do you work with your father?"

"This Saturday. It's part time. It's full time after I graduate in June. Well, I've got to go. I've got school," he said, walking back to his bike. "Again, thanks for the cupcakes. I'm sure we'll have them for lunch."

As he pedaled away, she called out, "Please say hello to your mother for me!"

"I will, Mrs. Morga."

Today's conversation was short and quick, just how he liked it.

The truth was she was the worst cook in the neighborhood, and everyone dreaded her baked offerings. Her culinary skills were so bad that the neighbors had taken to prophesying which meal had finally killed her husband. Personally, Tony's money was on her lasagna, which tasted like wet cardboard and ketchup. Poor Mrs. Morga had no idea that everyone made fun of her, or if she did, she preferred not to notice.

Tony made quick work of his last papers and double-timed it home. His sister Angela, who was the spitting image of their mother in both looks and personality, was in the backyard hanging laundry next to the fruit trees.

"Ha, ha, you're touching my underwear," he called out to her. He wheeled his bike into the garage and dumped the box of cupcakes in the trash.

Angela yelled back, "Shut up or I'll put holes in 'em!"

Inside, Tony plopped his last paper onto the counter and grabbed an apple from a bushel basket brimming with ripe fruit. His mother made the best applesauce in Los Angeles County—and probably the whole state. "Don't, you'll spoil your appetite," his mother scolded, as she flipped pancakes over a hot griddle. He winced, putting it back. *For Christ's sake, why am I still following her orders?*

His other sister was setting the table for breakfast. At six years of age, Caterina was a blossoming know-it-all. She was squeezing between the kitchen table and her mother's sewing machine, which was topped with a bolt of fabric for a new dress for Angela, when she could not contain her curiosity anymore. "Are you marrying Emilia today?"

"Huh?" Luckily, Tony was not eating the apple, or he would have choked on it.

His mother, whose pinched face matched her trim figure, chimed in, "Caterina, I got married when I was eighteen but not on my birthday. Give your brother some time. It's all right for men to marry when they're a bit older." She turned to her son. "Did everyone get a paper?"

"Yes, Mom." Every morning, it was the same question, day after day. Did everyone get a paper? If she cared that much, why did she not just do it herself? Of course, he would never ask her, lest he risked a smack across the mouth for talking back.

His mother then asked her next customary question. "How was

5

Mrs. Morga?"

"Fine. She made cupcakes. I dumped 'em in the trash."

"Don't do that," his mother frowned.

"Why? It's not like she'll find out."

Maria Piccinin rubbed her forehead and sighed. "Don't forget to tell Emilia to come at six."

"I told her yesterday," he said, escaping down the hall. The last person he wanted to talk about was Emilia.

Opening his bedroom door, he found his brother finishing his algebra homework in a panic. Marco was a major-league baseball player in the making. He was agile and quick for an eighth grader, and with his taller build he could hit with power. This season he had fifty-four runs batted in. "Hey Champ," Tony said, tossing the satchel to him, "there's no more sleep for you."

· Marco let the bag hit the floor. "Screw off, Birthday Boy!"

"Thanks," Tony smirked, flopping onto his bed. The room was decorated with baseball trophies and memorabilia, and the many photographs of his girlfriend, Emilia. Small frames, big frames—it seemed that every time Tony turned around, Emilia gave him another picture. She was the prettiest girl in school, that much was common knowledge, and any of the guys would give an arm or a leg, or maybe both, for a date with her, but Tony knew better. She was a tireless nag, a bothersome bore, and he was sick of it.

What was more, Emilia competed in everything—clothes, possessions, make-up, and even boyfriends. You name it; she had to have the best. Tony felt like aces at first. It was incredible. He was the envy of every guy at school. But soon, he realized the sorry truth. Every time he gave her a gift or took her on an expensive date, she expected the next present or evening to be better than the last. Before he knew it, he was taking on extra mowing jobs, painting houses, and trimming hedges just to have the cabbage to take her to nice places. But there was still no pleasing her, no matter how hard he tried. Sometimes, he wanted to just shake her by the shoulders and shout, "Can't you just enjoy what you have?"

Tony wanted out, but after he had bragged about Emilia in the beginning, he could not admit it to anyone, especially his brother, who had despised her from the start. Then there was his mother. He did not understand why, but she absolutely doted on Emilia. His girlfriend's wellbeing was like a full-time hobby to Maria, who asked about her relentlessly. Tony did not want to cross paths with his mother over Emilia. Ever!

Marco grabbed a notebook on his desk and opened it up to the page with two columns marked, "At Bats" and "Hits." "C'mon," he said, pencil poised. "Did Mom get a hit?"

Tony was glad for the distraction. "The bat?"

Marco got up and snatched a small wooden bat from under his bed, and Tony retrieved a rubber ball from his drawer. Tony lowered his voice as he mimicked the commentary of Mel Allen, the radio announcer for the New York Yankees. "Maria Sansone steps up to the plate, batting a whopping five-twenty-three. She out-hits the great Ted Williams, who bats a paltry four-o-six. Tony Piccinin winds up and throws a fast ball right down the middle." The boys used their mother's maiden name during these imaginary plays to distance themselves as far as possible from her weirdness.

Tony lobbed the ball, and Marco smacked it. Tony dodged, and the ball ricocheted off one of Emilia's photos, cracking the glass. "You shit!" Tony cried, as he tried to hide his amusement. "Look what you did!"

Marco laughed, and Tony returned to his announcer's voice. "Did everyone get a paper? Crack! For the four-thousandth time, Sansone connects with the sweet part of the bat. It's going— going— and it's gone!" Marco cupped his hands over his mouth and imitated the sound of a crowd cheering as he ran the bases in the cramped room. He touched the bed and dresser for second and third base, while Tony hammed it up. "For Tony Piccinin's last career pitch, Maria Sansone hit her eight hundred-and-twenty-seventh home run!"

Tomorrow it would be Marco's job to deliver the *Times* until he turned eighteen. Tony knew his brother would want to continue their morning ritual he concocted four years ago, after his mother had asked on the twentieth straight morning, "Did everyone get a paper?"

From the kitchen, their mother's voice rang out, "Boys, breakfast is ready!"

They fell over each other, panting and laughing. "We're coming, Mom."

Marco added a mark to each column and stored the notebook in his desk. They snagged their schoolbooks off their desks and raced from the room. Dumping their books on the sideboard, where four sack lunches awaited, the boys took their places at the kitchen table. "About time," Caterina reprimanded, pushing her glasses up her little nose.

Marco nudged Tony. "About time! Four eyes!"

Maria glared at her youngest son as she heaped four pancakes onto Tony's plate. "Marco, behave yourself!"

When their mother turned her back, Caterina stuck her tongue out at Marco, who punched and rubbed his fist, dramatizing her fate.

"So childish," Angela remarked, pouring the orange juice.

"Caterina, may I please have the milk?" Tony asked, thinking *all* his siblings were a tad immature. Yes, he enjoyed goofing with Marco in the bedroom, but it was time to get serious. After all, he would start his new job at Coca-Cola on Saturday.

Passing the pitcher, Caterina snickered, "I guess so, since it's your birthday and all!"

All at once, the family erupted, "*Buon Compleanno*! Happy Birthday!"

His mother kissed him on the cheek. "I love you," she said by his ear. "I'm so proud of you." She fixed his shirt collar and straightened his hair.

Marco punched Tony's bicep and leaned into him. "Just wait until tonight."

"What did you say?" Angela asked, sticking her nose where it did not belong, as usual.

"Nothin'," Marco and Tony chorused, stifling their smiles.

Chapter Two

After baseball practice and a shower, Tony slicked back his black hair and patted on just a hint of cologne. Wearing the white dress shirt his mother had made for the occasion, he emerged from his room to the aroma of her famous chicken cacciatore emanating from the kitchen.

The living room swung with the big band sounds of the Jimmy Dorsey Orchestra, as his father and grandfather debated over a glass of homemade wine whose band was better: Jimmy or Tommy Dorsey's. Tony noted the strains of 'Blue Champagne' coming from the radio cabinet. "*Buon Compleanno!*" Antonio sang out. He draped his arm around his son's shoulder and gave him a hearty kiss on the cheek. "You ready to join me on Saturday?" His father was rugged and handsome in his work clothes, but after working ten hours he could have used a drop or two of cologne himself.

"Of course he is," Grandpa Sansone said, pooh-poohing his son-in-law in his thick Italian accent that made his consonants sounded like vowels. "He's eighteen today, isn't he?" Smoothing back his thick gray hair, he reached out and rubbed Tony's shoulder affectionately. "How's the arm?" Tony was the star pitcher on his team for two years running with a combined record of twenty-five and three with two-hundred and thirteen strikeouts. He threw the fastball with plenty of smoke; as well as the curve ball, and change-up.

"It's fine," Tony replied.

While his father wanted him to deliver Coca-Cola for a living and his girlfriend and mother wanted him to propose, Tony had his heart set on playing minor league, then major league baseball for the Yankees. But first, he had to pitch in the playoffs on Thursday.

The doorbell rang, and Mrs. Piccinin, ever the perfect hostess in a green dress she had fashioned herself, answered the door. Emilia stood there, beaming at everyone. A few inches taller than his mother, she breezed in with her brunette hair flowing past her shoulders. At seventeen, she had the poise and confidence of a twenty-year-old.

She held her head high, never slouched or fidgeted, and in any conversation, she always talked with a purpose. Tony caught the scent of her perfume from across the room—French, of course. She had spent hours on her face, hair, clothes, and accessories, claiming she did it just for him, but he knew better.

From across the room, he watched his mother kiss Emilia on both cheeks and take her hands, admiring her dress, and for good reason. She wore a daytime party dress with a raised collar and matching heels. It looked fetching and sophisticated on her, even under Tony's letterman's jacket.

When she took the coat off, the dress accented her slim waist and beautiful face. "Dear, you look lovely," his mother said, appreciating her sense of fashion, though Tony had a suspicion the charming outfit showed more flesh than his mother thought was appropriate. "Tony, doesn't she look lovely?"

All eyes fell on him. Of course Emilia looked lovely. She had spent a small fortune on all the latest styles, plus she was gorgeous. "She always does," he said, eliciting Emilia's approving smile. *What else could I say?*

His mother turned to Angela and held out her hand. "Come see Emilia's dress."

Jesus, give it a rest! Everyone got it. Emilia was beautiful, she wore the right clothes, and his mother wanted him to marry her right away. But marriage was a long time to hear non-stop chatter about fashion and gossip about good people.

"Yes, Mother," Angela said, her ears burning red. His sister hated being compared to Emilia, but she knew better than to fret. "You do look pretty, Emilia."

Emilia basked in the praise. "Thank you. My aunt thinks I

should model. She says my skin tone would really show off the clothes."

Dear God, make it stop! Tony thought.

Angela did not say another word. She forced a smile, then disappeared into the kitchen. Across the room, Marco shook his head in disbelief. Breaking the awkward silence, as she guided Emilia to the sofa, Mrs. Piccinin asked, "How are your parents? It's been ages since I've seen your mother."

Setting her gift down, Emilia took a seat. "Oh, just fine. On Saturday, Mother and I are going dress shopping. You and Angela should come. We'll have lunch at the Brown Derby."

Reappearing, Angela sidled up to her mother. "Oh, can we Mother? I'd love to have a store-bought dress for the Hallowe'en Dance. I could go as Dorothy!" Both Tony and Marco rolled their eyes. Every girl, including their little sister, wanted to dress up as Dorothy since the release of *The Wizard of Oz*.

"We'll see," Mrs. Piccinin said. The four siblings knew that meant no. Their mother changed the subject. "Dinner isn't ready yet. Why don't we open the presents now?"

Emilia took her gift-wrapped box and shoved it into Tony's hand. "Mine first!" She beamed with so much pride; it was a miracle she did not burst.

Odds were one to ten that it was a photograph of her, a sure thing. Tony wanted to take bets, he knew all about odds. He and his brother loved to accompany their grandfather to the horse track. Santa Anita was a change of pace for them, bumping shoulders with the sharpies and not having to mind their language.

He removed the wrapping, opened the box, and just as expected, another picture of Emilia lay inside. "Oh, how lovely," said his mother. "Show us." Tony turned it around for a few seconds, showing everyone, and placed it on the table without a word.

"Do you like it?" Emilia asked, fluttering her eyelashes at him.

"Yes. It's nice," he said, reaching for the next present and hoping to move things along.

But his mother picked up the framed photo and gushed, "This is just *darling*! You are so photogenic, Emilia."

"Thank you," Emilia said, sitting up straighter. "It took three sittings to get it right." She turned back to Tony. Her perfect features were marred by a slight frown. "Don't you like it? I was thinking about you the whole time."

His mother glanced at him with a raised eyebrow. It was clear she wanted more from him than just 'Yes, it's nice'. Doing his best to appease them both, Tony pulled out a big smile. "Of course, it's great. I know just right where I'm gonna put it so I can gaze upon your beauty all the time." He hoped that sounded sincere.

Satisfied with his answer, his mother set the photograph back into his hands.

With a sense of relief, Emilia inched closer to Tony and gawked at her own picture. "Do you like the dress? It's a Barcelona evening dress. My aunt bought it for me at Katharine's Boutique in New York City. Do you like the ruffles in the shoulders?"

Unable to resist, Marco jumped in. "It's just lovely, Emilia." He said it in a tone that was hard to discern between sarcasm and sincerity, but his family knew better.

Mr. Piccinin stared at Marco. It was his way of warning his youngest son. And Mrs. Piccinin ignored the comment and carried on the conversation. "Emilia, the drape on that dress is perfect."

"Thank you, Mrs. Piccinin." Smiling, Emilia was oblivious to everything else.

Tony opened his parents' presents next—a Coca-Cola work shirt and two pairs of work pants. He really wanted a new baseball bat or glove, anything other than work clothes. Tony held up the pants, and his mother admonished him. "Make sure everything fits."

"Yeah, that's a good idea," Marco said. "Try on your pants in front of your girlfriend!" Tony reached across Caterina and socked him on the arm. "Ow! What's that for?" Marco rubbed his arm, and Mrs. Piccinin gave her oldest child one of her looks.

"Here, you forgot one," Grandpa said. He walked over with a

slight stoop and handed Tony a thin package wrapped in newspaper. He took it, and his mood improved right away. His grandfather always gave him the best gifts. He was the only person who understood what made him tick. He unwrapped the package. Inside was the 1941 World Series Program.

Tony opened the cover carefully, admiring each page and its shiny gloss.

"Thanks, Grandpa." Tony got up and hugged him. He rotated it around to show everyone and pointed to the cover. "Look! It's signed: *Amore*, Giuseppe DiMaggio. That's amazing!"

Marco shot out a hand to grab the program, but Mrs. Piccinin jumped forward. "Don't, your hands are dirty."

"Huh? Mom, I just washed them," he said.

Emilia wriggled in her seat as though her bottom was on fire. Obviously, she was peeved that Tony found this gift more appealing than hers. "Who's Giuseppe?" she asked, as though the name had a bad taste to it.

"Joe DiMaggio, that's who," Marco said.

"And who's that?" Emilia asked, without a trace of irony.

Everyone except Maria laughed in disbelief.

How in heaven's name can she not know who Joe DiMaggio is? And she's an Italian! In this family, Joltin' Joe came second only to Pope Pius XII, and for some, maybe a little above the Pope. Tony supposed she could not help being a girl, but still, she should know who Joe DiMaggio was.

He tried to explain. "He's only the best baseball player ever. This season he had a hit in fifty-six straight games. You know him, Emilia. I talk about him all the time."

"Oh yes, now I know who you're talking about," Emilia faked. She pursed her lips; a sure sign of her disinterest.

He wondered why they were still dating. They had nothing in common, really. Her dad was a movie financier, whereas his dad delivered soda. She wore the latest fashions; his mom made most of their clothes. Her friends were sophisticated with wealthy parents; his were simple and crass with part-time jobs, before or after school—and sometimes both. At first, Tony was flattered that Emilia had shown an interest in him. They went to their junior prom together and had been exclusive ever since. Everyone assumed they would get married after graduation.

But for months, Tony had been busy crafting an escape route. He begged off more and more dates and spent less and less time with Emilia and her crowd, hoping she would get the hint. Unfortunately, she never did. In fact, she talked more and more about their future together. He felt the distinct pull of a noose tightening around his neck, and he did not know how to escape.

Tony wanted to tell his parents that Emilia was stuck-up and spoiled, but he knew they would not understand. To them, she and her family were the very definition of class. But still, how could he marry her? She did not even know who Joe DiMaggio was!

Tony looked around the living room at his family and girlfriend as they chatted. He was eighteen now, no longer a boy. It was time to be a man. If he only knew what that meant!

Chapter Three

A hush fell over the field as Tony reared his arm back and released the baseball. His arm extended so far from the effort that his fingers nearly dusted the mound before he righted himself and followed the ball's trajectory. The batter stood over the plate, bat up, as the ball sailed straight past him. "Stee-rike!" the umpire said, spitting a stream of tobacco juice into a dry puddle at his feet.

It was the bottom of the second inning of the semi-finals of the Los Angeles High School Championship, and Tony's temper was climbing higher than the sun. He had not slept the night before, hoping a baseball scout would be watching him pitch. His parochial school was up against a city team, the Jefferson Eagles, an all-Japanese school located in Boyle Heights.

His catcher, Innis McDowell, tossed the ball back to him. He was a chubby Irish kid with a mop of reddish hair and freckles splashed across his wide, pressed-in nose. "Keep 'em coming, Tony," he drawled. "Keep 'em coming."

Tony did just that. One, two more strikes for the third out, and the rest of the team followed him off the field and into the dugout for the Bishop Chatard Cougars.

Coach Grazziano, a handsome algebra teacher whom all the girls called Ga-Ga Grazziano, readjusted his cap several times. "Seven more innings like that, and we'll be home for afternoon tea." Good looking with a nervous habit he was, funny he was not.

In his favorite corner of the dugout, Tony paced, cursing himself for his lackluster performance. Sure, they were up 2-0 after two, but the Eagles were better than he had anticipated. He had given up three hits, and his shoulder was sore. He had seven innings to go. "What gives?" Innis asked. "I thought a few of them were gonna leave without their heads."

Tony kicked the dirt with his cleats and scoffed, "It's their own damn fault. If they don't back off, I'm gonna take a couple of them out."

Innis turned and hung his hands on the chain-link fence. "C'mon, Aldo. Get a hit."

Tony studied the pitcher. Tak Fujiyana was tall and thin, not an ounce of fat on him. His style was the antithesis to Tony's hot-blooded method of pitching, wind 'em up and let 'em go. Whereas Tony grunted and sweated each strike, Tak threw like a Zen monk, barely flinching as he let each ball fly, true to its course.

"That Jap sure has an arm on him," Innis grunted.

Tony winced. "Do you have to call 'em that?"

"What? Japs? That's what everyone calls 'em," Innis stated.

"Yeah, just like everybody calls you Mick or Paddy and me Dago or Guinea!"

"I don't mind it. I kind of like it," he smiled, spitting at the ground.

"Well, I don't. So cut it out." Out of the corner of his eye, Tony could tell Innis was giving him a long, hard stare, but he did not care.

* * * * *

It was the bottom of the fifth with two outs. Behind some bad fielding, the Cougars had extended their lead, five to one. Yuji Geikkekan, the Eagles' second baseman and best hitter, was up. While he was small in stature, he had broad shoulders and railroad ties for forearms. Famous for his home runs, Yuji stood over the plate liked he owned it.

The Eagles had encroached on his territory long enough. Tony zeroed in on his catcher and refused Innis's sign before agreeing on an inside fastball. With perfect precision, his pitch sailed from his hand

and beaned Yuji in the upper arm, and when they did not get the message to back off the plate, Tony plunked a batter in both the sixth and eighth inning.

In the top of the ninth, Tony was on deck, and the score was five to two. He swung his bat to loosen out his sore arm. If he was ever going to sleep tonight, he needed an ice bath, followed by a hot shower and one of his mother's shoulder rubs. Ahead of him, Patrick Adams stood poised and ready, until a fastball flew right over the middle of the plate for his third strike.

"Take a seat," the umpire muttered. From the way he said it, Tony knew he was fed up and ready to go home.

Tony wiped his sweaty palms on his pants and stepped up to the plate. He felt the tension from the Eagles' side of the stands. He set up in the back of the box and away from the plate, giving the pitcher plenty of room, the way a batter should. He squinted at the mound, his bat high off his shoulder, elbows up, and the Eagle's second baseman yelled to the pitcher, *"Karo o hensai!"*

Tak nodded, wound up, and threw the ball hard. Tony arched his back, missing the bullet by a fraction of a second. "Ball one!" the umpire snapped, as the catcher chuckled.

Tony stepped back to the plate. This time the shortstop screeched, *"Kare o molte ikou!"*

Again, the Eagle's pitcher nodded at his teammate's instruction, and Tony braced for whatever was coming. Tak wound up and threw a fastball, high and inside. Tony fell backwards, and his cap toppled to the ground. "Ball two!" the ump shouted.

"Dammit," Tony complained, picking up his cap and banging off a cloud of brown dust against his leg. He sneered at the ump, "He's trying to hit me."

The umpire fired back, "Quit your whining. You beaned three of them."

But Tony stood his ground. "Yeah, they had it coming! They crowded the plate! I'm not crowding nothin'."

The Eagles coach stepped out of the dugout and yelled to Tak.

"*Kare o toru!*"

Tony did not know what was said, but the tone of the man's voice and the look on his face told him it was not pretty.

The players and the fans for the Jefferson Eagles started chanting. "*Kare o toru! Kare o toru! Kare o toru!*"

"Batter up!" the ump said.

While Tony stepped into the batter's box and bent into position, he heard his teammate Sal Giannini start with the insults. "No good Jap!"

"Yellow coward!" another jeered.

Tony did not know what pissed him off more—Tak's pitching tactics or his teammates being complete dumbasses. He did his best to push their taunts out of his mind as he watched Tak wind up. He braced. Bam! Another high and inside fastball. Tony ducked just in time, and the catcher barely managed to get his glove on the ball. "Ball three!" the umpire shouted.

Tony turned to him, his hands out wide. "What the hell? He's aiming at me!"

The ump pointed a finger at him. "Watch your mouth! They're no worse than yours."

In disbelief, Tony glared at the umpire, then at Tak, who stood with his head slightly tilted to one side, a placid smile upon his face. That was all it took. Tony pointed his bat at him. "Do it again, and I'm kicking your ass!"

"Fighting is a forfeit!" the umpire warned.

* * * * *

In the bleachers, Marco and Grandpa soaked in every move and gesture. The whole family was there except his dad, who had to work. While they knew Tony had a temper, Marco had never seen him this livid before. "Look, Grandpa, he's gonna blow. I can tell."

Caterina looked up from her book. "Not again."

Grandpa cupped his hands at his mouth and called out, "Tony, stay calm. This one's in the bag."

Marco bit his nails and spit the fragments out with perfect precision.

Suddenly, Emilia, drowning in Tony's oversized letterman's jacket, forced her way up the packed stands to where the Piccinins sat for every game. Marco, wishing she would vamoose, groaned as she wiggled her way into their row and tossed her hair. "Hi, did I miss anything?" she asked.

Marco stared forward. "Not much. It's just the top of the ninth."

"Phew, I'm in time for the last quarter." She sat down, and a cloud of French perfume settled around her, causing a few heads to turn.

"It's innings, not quarters!" Marco's eyes shot daggers at her.

"You sure? At the football game, Tony said quarters."

Marco threw his hands up in defeat. "You got me there."

Emilia ignored him and waved to Angela, Caterina, and Mrs. Piccinin at the other end. "I love your dress," Mrs. Piccinin said, beaming with pride in front of the other mothers.

Emilia stood back up and opened up her jacket so she and all the ladies in the stands could get a better view of her romper day dress with dual pockets. "Thank you. It was a Christmas present from my uncle and his wife in Washington D.C. You know, he works at the State Department."

Marco groaned. Why did girls come to a baseball game to talk about dresses? He sighed, wishing he could make Emilia disappear.

A few rows back, a man bellowed, "Down in front!"

Emilia gazed up at the man, and Marco knew she was wondering what was wrong with him. She arranged her dress and jacket just so, then sat down again.

* * * * *

Tony stepped back in the batter's box and held his bat up. His face was on fire; he could feel it. Tak gripped the ball and wound up for the pitch. He launched it straight for his head. Tony's eyes were glued to the spinning ball, absorbing every detail, from the smudges of brown dirt to the red stitching, as it zoomed toward him. At the last split-second he hit the dirt.

"Ball four! Take your—" But before the umpire could finish, Tony charged the mound, blind rage pumping through his veins. Frozen in fear, Tak stood still, his eyes bulging and the blood draining from his face. With a sickening thud, Tony rammed into him and took him to the ground. As Tak lay flat on his back, Tony's fists pummeled into him again and again. Yes, this would cost his team a chance at the city championship, and if there was a scout in the stands, it would be embarrassing. But he simply did not care anymore. This guy deserved it.

Both benches emptied, and Tony's teammates pulled him off the battered pitcher. Without warning, Tak jumped up, cocked his arm back, and threw a punch to Tony's face, but Patrick blocked it with his forearm. Innis grabbed Tak's left arm, twisting it and cursing, "Damn Jap!"

"Typical Jap cheating!" Patrick shouted, as he secured Tak's right arm.

"You can't trust them!" Sal shoved Tak forward, so Tony could hit him again.

Suddenly, Tony felt the pain in Tak's eyes and backed up, shaking his head. What was he doing? He did not like the look in Patrick's eyes,'s fervent zeal, nor the veins pulsing on either side of Sal's neck. He caught hold of his breathing and bent at the waist. "Whoa, whoa, guys. Hey, it's not like that! Let him go. I said let him go!"

His teammates loosened their grips on Tak, and the fight broke up. Tony grabbed the Eagles' pitcher's forearm, pulled him in close, and to Tak's surprise, instructed him on how to bean a batter. "Don't telegraph it. You hear me? Outside then inside. You got it? One shot!"

The umpire separated the teams and called the game. Bishop

Chatard forfeited for fighting. They were three outs away from victory. Tony looked up and scanned the stands. Meeting the eyes of his despairing brother and disappointed grandfather, he gave a faint shrug.

Now, it was up to Marco to win the city championship for Grandpa.

Chapter 4

Standing in front of the mirror, the red-and-white striped Coca-Cola work shirt looked snazzy on him. With his name embroidered over his left breast pocket and his hair combed just right, Tony thought he could pass for a manager at Coca-Cola or at the least a shift supervisor. He straightened the collar and rechecked himself once more.

Having finished his paper route, Marco lounged on his bed, browsing the latest edition of *Captain America*. A typical eighth grader, he was spending his money faster than he was earning it. "I bet it's hard work," he commented.

"It beats delivering papers every morning," Tony replied. "It's easy money." But in truth Tony was not all that sure about his new job. What if he broke a bottle—or worse dropped a whole crate of bottles and they busted—would they take it out of his paycheck? What if he wrecked the truck? Would he have to deliver Coca-Cola for free, forever, just to pay it off? Now his old newspaper route did not seem so bad in comparison.

Marco turned a page in his comic book. "The only easy money I know is free, and they aren't paying you for doing nothing."

"God, are you back to your stupid ideas and free money?" He slid his Coca-Cola cap on, taking care not to undo all his hard work on his hair.

"Just wait. Someday I'll be one of those robber barons."

"That'll be the day." Tony gave his reflection one last admiring look before he headed toward the living room where final inspection awaited him.

From her place next to Angela, his mother arose from the sofa. "You look handsome," she said, her voice somewhat strained. She pinched her son's shoulders and tugged on his sleeves. "How does it fit? Anything too tight? Too loose? I can always let it out."

"It's fine. Where's Dad?"

"Outside."

He mustered a smile. "I've got to go."

"You look good," his mother said.

"Thanks. You always say that."

Angela noticed the glassiness in her mother's eyes. "Mom, he's not going off to war! It's just work."

Mrs. Piccinin let out a heavy sigh. "I know, but dad's first day seems like yesterday."

Tony kissed his mother on the cheek, then raced outside, wondering if he too would still be delivering Coke twenty years from now. He climbed into the family car, and Mr. Piccinin pulled out of the driveway. "Did Mom give you a hard time?"

"You know it," Tony said, sharing a laugh with his father.

"Now you know why I always wait in the car."

* * * * *

At the Coca-Cola bottling plant his father introduced Tony around, and everyone welcomed the new recruit with handshakes and hard pats on the back. The Piccinin men loaded their truck with crates of soda. Leaving the warehouse, the rattles, shakes, and clanks of the bottles grew louder with each bump in the road.

They had already made three stops when they pulled up to Kashiwagi's Korner Market, a two-story, business-residential building at the corner of Jefferson Boulevard and Figueroa Street. The University of Southern California was across the boulevard. Written on the lower windows were the specials for the week: bacon eleven cents per pound, ground beef fifteen cents per pound, and flour nineteen cents for four pounds. Colorful fall leaves decorated the advertisements. On the second floor, florid drapes fluttered in the open windows.

Tony and his father hustled out of the truck and loaded a dolly with cases of Coca-Cola. Mr. Piccinin leaned over. "This guy knows what he's doing. I met him out on Terminal Island and he became my first client. Now he has five stores, and this is his best one. These college kids need snacks and drinks, and he cleans up. I'm telling you, I'm in the wrong business."

Tony allowed his dad's words and frank manner to sink in. It seemed like he was no longer a kid who needed to mind his own beeswax while the adults were talking, but more like he was now an adult himself—even perhaps, a friend.

"Nice store," Tony said, reaching for another crate of bottles.

"I'll say." His father looked up at the second floor. "His family lives up there."

* * * * *

In the store's back office, Yoshimitsu Kashiwagi, a middle-aged Japanese-American man in a tailored suit, was in the middle of a conversation with Herbert Schultz, a Los Angeles City Councilman and owner of two corner grocery stores himself. He was accompanied by his son Jeff, a junior at USC. Mr. Schultz was making an unsolicited offer for his five stores.

"Mr. Kashywaguy," he began, mispronouncing his name as most people did, "the tide is turning. With Japan allied to Germany and Italy, it's only a matter of time before you are at war with the United States. And then you won't be able to give your stores away."

The room was small and clean, with a few shelves containing notebooks and ledgers. Mr. Kashiwagi stood at his desk staring at the man and his son. They wanted to purchase his stores and pull the rug from right under his chair. And then what? Where would he go? He had owned his stores for twenty years, and now, because of the war in Europe, they thought they could take advantage of him.

"Mr. Schultz, I understand what you are saying, but my country is the United States. If what you say is true, I'm not worried. I'm an American. Japan, Germany, it doesn't matter where I'm from or where you're from. We're Americans now. Nothing will happen to me."

Mr. Schultz turned to his son and shrugged. "C'mon Jeff. You can't help those who don't want to be helped." He stopped at the doorway and turned toward Mr. Kashiwagi once more, warning him. "You better think this over before it's too late."

As they left, Mr. Kashiwagi slumped into his chair, letting go of the breath he had been holding for some time.

* * * * *

A cowbell clanged overhead as Mr. Piccinin opened the front door for Tony, who pushed in the dolly stacked with bottles of Coke. A Japanese girl stood behind the cash register, catching Tony by surprise. The Japanese did not live on this side of town. She was chatting to two male students who were dressed in cardinal and gold for the USC football game against Stanford that afternoon. On a shelf above her, a radio played 'Scrub Me, Mama, With a Boogie Beat' by the Andrews Sisters.

Tony hauled the dolly to the display rack of Coca-Cola, as he listened to their conversation.

"I heard about Waterman's test. You ready?" The girl spoke without a Japanese accent.

"I better be," one of the guys said. "It's been one, two o'clock every night."

"What about you?" she asked the other guy.

Tony was mesmerized by the unpretentious way this girl carried herself. Unlike Emilia, she seemed not to care if she looked her best, or if her hair was just right, or if her lipstick was on just so. Instead she just leaned on her elbows and talked to the customers, smiling as though she had known them for years.

"That's right. You take the old bottles out, put the new bottles in, and then you place the old bottles on top," his father said, drowning out the other guy's reply.

"You're so smart. I don't know how you guys do it!" the girl exclaimed.

Tony caught another glimpse of her as he grabbed a case of soda, taking in her brown eyes and white teeth. Her skin had a beautiful, soft sheen.

As the guys were leaving, she called out, "Don't forget your change! And good luck with your exam on Monday. I know you'll do well." This doll made his head spin—a pleasant personality and a genuine interest in others. Was she always this delightful?

Unaware of his son's new interest, Mr. Piccinin continued with his instructions. "That's it. It should look just like that with the trademark on display."

Tony wished his dad would stop supervising and just let him do his thing. He emptied the dolly and put the old bottles back on top, just as the girl emerged from behind the counter to tidy a few of the shelves. She wore a white cotton blouse that accentuated her small waist and a blue knit skirt, fashionable but not rakish.

Mr. Piccinin turned to her with a friendly smile. "Hello, Amy. This is my son, Tony. Today's his first day."

"Hi," Tony said, trying not to stare at her. But she caught him. She smiled, showing off those perfect white teeth, and he tore his gaze away. *Dammit! Can't you keep your act together for one minute?*

"It's nice to meet you. I hear you're a pitcher?"

"Well, yes, I am," he replied, giving his father a sly look. So he had been talking about me. *Wait, God, I'm so dumb! Terminal Island, the sign outside—the owner is Japanese and this is his daughter. How old is she?*

"Does the cooler need refilling?" Mr. Piccinin asked Amy.

When she turned to check, her skirt twirled. She had long, slender calves that disappeared into short white socks and black and white Mary Janes. "Mr. Piccinin, thank you, but no thanks." *What was that? Thank you, but no thanks. Damn! What a nobby way to say no.*

"Is your dad in back?" his father asked.

"Yes, Mr. Piccinin."

"I'll be back," he said to Tony.

At that moment two men, one much older than the other, strutted out of the office. The older man saw Tony's father and smiled with a grimace. "Antonio, how are you?" he asked, extending his hand.

His father shook it firmly. "Mr. Schultz, it's good to see you. How are you?"

"Fine," he beamed, "couldn't be better. You remember my boy, Jeff?"

"Sure. How are you, Jeff?" Mr. Piccinin shook hands with Jeff, who said nothing. His father turned his attention back to Herbert Schultz. "So, you know Mr. Kashiwagi? I had no idea."

Mr. Schultz glanced back at Mr. Kashiwagi's open door. "You could say we're just getting acquainted."

"Well, he's a good guy to know," Mr. Piccinin said.

He studied Mr. Piccinin for a second, then clapped him on the shoulder. "Indeed. I'll see you on Tuesday."

Tony watched as the two Schultzs, who shared the same build and gait, headed toward the front door. Amy was on her toes, dusting the sacks of flour on the top shelf, when Jeff, who wore a USC letterman's jacket he got for cross-country, stopped to admire her from behind. "Hey, good looking, how are you?"

She pivoted. Her face stiffened. "Hi, Jeff."

Mr. Schultz scowled at his son. "Let's go!"

Jeff smirked at his father's impatience and winked at Amy. "I'll see you later." Then he noticed Tony watching. "Hey, Coke Boy, keep your peepers to yourself."

With the cowbell clanking, he swaggered out.

"Don't let him bother you," Amy said. "He's all hogwash."

"Ain't that the truth," Tony said. And the two of them laughed.

As she resumed her dusting, the radio played a Benny Goodman tune, 'Stompin' at the Savoy', and her hips swayed to the music ever so slightly.

He pushed the dolly out of the aisle. "Do you like Goodman?"

Her movement stopped, and without turning around, Amy said, "He's keen. You hop?"

Hop? Of course he did. Emilia would kill him, though, if he admitted it to another girl, but it was all the encouragement he needed. With a frog in his throat, Tony said, "I'm smooth."

She spun around, her face lighting up. "Really?"

He stood a little taller. She was getting prettier by the second. He could not deny it. "Yes, really. You jitterbug?"

Amy cocked her head ever so slightly and leaned back against the shelf, smiling playfully. "I'm the best in LA."

Loving a good challenge, Tony stepped forward, matching her smile with his own. "Excuse me, but you're second best."

Just then the music stopped, and the disc jockey announced, "Next up for all you Jitterbugs is a new one by Alvino Rey, 'Deep in the Heart of Texas'."

Tony loved that song. He had bought the record just the other day. As the song began its infectious melody, Amy waggled her hands at her hips. "Second best?" She teased. "You're right. There's Cary Grant. I'd love to rag with him."

This girl was murder. She was not high on herself at all—more like a fun-spirited quality Tony could not quite describe. He placed his left hand on the display case to look calm and collected, but really, he needed to steady himself. "Do you go to Southern Cal?"

"SC?" She laughed lightly, brushing her hair back. "I'm a senior at Manual."

"You're a senior at Manual?" Tony asked, thinking a babe like this had to be older. But he did know the school. He had played them in baseball.

"Why? Is there a problem?" Amy smiled at him.

He loved the way she challenged him. She was testing him and at the same time flirting. This tomato had all the angles. "No. None what-so-ever."

The cowbell over the door broke up the conversation. Two college-looking girls walked in, and Amy left to wait on them. One was a blonde and the other one was a brunette. Both were lookers by anyone's standards, but as far as Tony was concerned, they were no match for Amy.

* * * * *

In the back office, Mr. Kashiwagi wrote a check from his ledger and handed it to Antonio. "Is that correct?"

"Yes, sir, as always." Antonio folded the check and slid it into his shirt pocket. "Can I tell you something?"

"What is it, Mr. Piccinin?"

"You know how highly I think of you." He hesitated, glancing around to see if anyone was listening. "That Mr. Schultz is rotten to the core. I had to switch him to cash only, and it isn't because he doesn't have the money. He has it all right and plenty of it, but he can't be trusted. Some time ago, he made a pact with the Devil, and he likes his side of the bargain."

Mr. Kashiwagi sat there, listening without moving, absorbing every word.

"I just thought you should know."

"Thank you Mr. Piccinin. You've been looking out for me for a long time. Well, if it wasn't for your tip that Mrs. Kauffman was selling, I never would've bought this place fifteen years ago. I appreciate your advice.

* * * * *

At last, the cowbell rang, marking the exit of the two college girls. Tony cleared his throat and drifted over to Amy. His palms were sweaty, just like in a baseball game whenever he moved from the on deck circle to the batter's box, and his heart felt like it was beating in his throat. "So, um, my high school is having a Hallowe'en dance next Friday. Would—"

Suddenly, he heard his father's footsteps on the wooden floor, and Tony tried to take his swing before it was too late. "Would you—"

His father interrupted, "Amy, take care. Tony, the dolly."

Tony's shoulders slumped as he grabbed the dolly and followed his father out the door.

Amy called after him. "Have a good time at your dance!"

Chapter 5

"How was it? Tough?" Marco asked, as he leafed through an issue of *True Comics*.

Tony cricked his neck, then straightened his baseball sleeves. "Naw, not too bad. Everyone was keen."

The bedroom door opened, and Paul sauntered in, carrying a baseball glove and cleats. His cheeks were flush from running, and like Tony and his brother, he wore baseball sleeves, jeans, and sneakers. He dropped his stuff onto Tony's bed. "You should've told me sooner. *High Sierra* was murder."

"I told ya. Bogart is aces. But you wouldn't listen." Tony hunched his broad shoulders, squinted his blue eyes, and gave his best Humphrey Bogart impersonation. "You got it all figured out, ain't you?"

Paul yanked the comic from Marco's hand and collapsed onto the bed. "Not bad. Marco, what's your mom batting?"

"Like shit. Her head isn't in the game."

"You crack me up. What does she say?"

Marco imitated his mother's tone and pitch. "Did everyone get a paper?"

Paul laughed as he flipped through the comic book. "Hey, are we still doubling on Hallowe'en?"

"I don't know. I, uh—" Tony hesitated, looking down for a moment. "I met someone new."

Marco and Paul both stopped what they were doing and looked

31

at each other, eyes widening and smiles slowly materializing on their faces. Paul threw the comic back at Marco. "Who's the tomato?" he asked.

"She works by SC," Tony said, using Amy's lingo.

"By Southern Cal?" Paul asked.

"Yeah, by SC, you dipshit!"

Paul got up and slugged Marco's shoulder. "Foreign territory. I like it. Is she better than Emilia? You know—" He raised his eyebrows at Tony.

Marco slugged him back. "What're you, stupid?"

"He's right," Paul said. "Emilia is so Fifth Avenue, it makes me puke." With a hand to his waist and a high-pitched voice, he mimicked Emilia. "Look at my new blouse! It's from a Parisian boutique. Look at my shoes! They were cobbled in Milan." Paul cracked himself up, and then he turned to Tony. "C'mon, let's go ask her to the dance."

"What?" Tony asked.

Paul was undeterred. "Don't be a palooka. Your dad can—"

"It's not that easy," Tony interrupted. "She's Japanese."

"So what?" He hesitated for a second, building his case. "Marco, do you care—"

"Heck no. A three-armed Japanese gorilla would be better than Emilia."

Paul and Marco burst out laughing. "See? What are you waiting for? Just ditch her already!"

"I can't. My mom—"

"Jeez, don't be a Valvano!" Paul said, comparing Tony to the perpetual momma's boy in their Latin class.

Tony shot up and grabbed Paul around the neck. He was serious, but he was also playing at the same time. "What's wrong with you? Can't you just can it for once? I swear it won't kill you!"

"Jeez, aren't you touchy today?" Paul broke free from his grip. "C'mon, let's skiddle."

Tony surveyed his friend, a wry expression on his face. Paul had been his best buddy since kindergarten and he could never stay mad at him for long. Laughing, despite himself, he turned and headed for the door. "God, you're a pain in the ass."

* * * * *

The cowbell sounded as Tony and Paul entered Kashiwagi's Korner Market, but they could hardly hear it. Five SC jocks recounted the afternoon's game, blow by blow, while Amy leaned against the counter, listening.

At first, Tony felt like an intruder, but all that changed when Amy caught sight of him. To his surprise—and the chagrin of the five jocks—she slid away from the cluster and rushed straight to him. "Tony, we won! Twenty-four to ten."

Tony hardly heard the score. She had remembered his name! "That's great!" he said, turning to his buddy. "Amy, this is Paul Romano."

"What's buzzin'?" she asked, with a big smile on her face.

"Nothin', cuzzin'," Paul replied, without missing a beat.

They all laughed.

"Parched? Cokes?" Amy asked. "It's my treat."

"Thanks," Tony said, wondering what Paul thought of her.

"That'd be swell," Paul added.

While Amy grabbed two bottles of soda from the cooler, Paul whispered to Tony, "She's a doll, man. You've got to do this—"

"I know. But how?"

"Don't know. But if you don't I will."

Tony elbowed him in the chest. "Bite your lip, boy."

On her way back, one of the SC jocks bent her ear. "Hey Amy, how'd you like that return to start the second half?"

This girl was incredible. Wherever she turned, some guy was eating out of the palm of her hand.

"That was keen. Ninety-five yards up the right side, and they didn't come within ten feet of him," Amy replied to the guy towering over her. She reached into her pocket and pulled out two nickels, dropping them into the cash register drawer.

Smiling, she drifted away and handed Tony and Paul their bottles of Coca-Cola, but the big palooka followed. "But that Hail Mary pass," the guy said, "now that was amazing."

When Amy made eye contact with Tony, he saw his opportunity. "So Amy, for my school's Hallowe'en Dance—"

Without warning, the rest of the group surrounded them, yelling and shouting like they had the run of the place. God forbid a customer or her father should come in. "That run by Phillips in the third quarter, man. That danced!" one guy cried.

"Yeah. But that tackle by Dobbs sealed it!" another one shouted.

In the midst of this mayhem, Tony put his fingers into the corners of his lips and whistled like a freight train; a handy skill his grandpa had taught him. Everyone covered their ears and gawked at him. This was not exactly how he had imagined it going, but he had to do it. He turned to Amy. "Would you like to go to my school's Hallowe'en Dance?"

The room fell silent. Amy's fingertips were plugged into her ears, as she tried to get the ringing to stop. *Now what?*

"With me, I mean," he added, swallowing a lump that had formed in his throat.

No one moved, especially Amy. She just stood there, her beautiful eyes wide. *Is she going to answer? Dammit! This is so embarrassing.*

"Did you hear me?" Tony asked, trying again.

Dead silence.

"It's next Friday. If you're—" Tony could not find the rest of his words. *What are you—a complete dumbass, asking her like this?*

Paul clasped a hand on his shoulder. "Man, it's okay. You tried."

Now that he had made a complete fool of himself, a swift retreat was his only option. Tony and Paul turned and headed to the front door.

At the entranceway, they heard an imperceptible whisper.

"I'd—"

It was just enough to stop them. "I'd love to, Tony," Amy repeated softly.

When Tony turned back around, her smile was sweet, but sweeter still were the faces of the SC jocks staring at him, their eyes wide with surprise and perhaps a smidgen of admiration too.

Grinning from ear to ear, Tony let out a whistle that cleared out the store.

* * * * *

"So when are you going to tell Emilia?" Paul asked as Tony drove his father's car back home.

"I don't know." He looked sideways at Paul for a second. "And don't you go saying anything. You hear me? I'll tell her tonight. Hell, you know she'll blow! I'll take it. I have to; every word. That's how it'll go. Then she'll act— I got it! I got it! You know— like in the movies where the boy gets the girl. Boy loses girl. Then the boy gets the girl back. I'll just tell Emilia this is just a temporary phase we're going through, where I lose her. And if our love is true, I'll fight to get her back."

"It'll work." Paul grinned. "She's delusional!"

Chapter 6

Dressed as a nurse with white stockings and matching shoes, Amy sat in front of a tall, oval mirror that was surrounded by postcards. A wide dresser, with an opening in the middle for a chair and drawers on both sides for her clothes, brushes and makeup, doubled as her vanity and desk.

She could not decide whether to pin her hair up or leave it down. She settled on a tight bun, a classic look for a nurse. Struggling to fix the nurse's cap to her hair, Amy reached for a Japanese stickpin. Four inches long with a brass hummingbird design, it had been a gift from her mother on her eighteenth birthday. The heirloom had belonged to her grandmother, whom she had never met. She slid the pin through her hair, turned it around, and secured the cap in place.

Suddenly, Amy became aware of a presence standing in the doorway. Her mother's hair was perfectly coiffed, nails manicured, and her wrap dress with a floral print was crisp and newly ironed. Maki Kashiwagi smiled at her daughter. "I'm glad you're wearing Mother's pin. She'd be so excited for your first dance."

Amy stood, so her mother could see her costume.

"My old uniform! You look wonderful. I remember those days well."

June, Amy's sixteen-year-old sister, appeared from behind their mother to peer at her sister who was readjusting her cap. "Do you think he'll like it?" Amy asked.

Mrs. Kashiwagi laughed, "Of course he will."

"Is he blind?" June asked.

"Don't be silly," Amy giggled.

"Then he's gonna love it," June said, hugging her mother's waist, as Amy smiled at her sister affectionately. "Oh, I do wish I could go, Mother. May I *please?*"

"We already went through this, June," her mother said in a firm voice. "You know the rules. No dates until you're eighteen."

"It doesn't have to be a date, just a dance," June pleaded, "*Please?*"

"I'll think about it," their mother replied.

Amy gave June a sympathetic tilt of her head. Did her mother even remember what it was like when she was younger, having to wait so long just to attend a school dance? *What was the big deal?*

"What about me? Can I go?" Another face emerged under her mother's arm. Kelly, who had just turned nine, was dressed as a ballerina in a pink leotard and tutu, and white tights and ballet slippers.

"You wish," June said. "I'm taking you and your friend trick-or-treating, and when we get back, I'm eating all the candy."

"No!" Kelly shrieked.

There was a knock at the front door. Amy's heart began to pound. "He's here," she whispered.

"He's here!" June yelled through the house.

"Stop, he'll hear you!" Amy chastised her sister.

But Kelly was already racing down the hall, crying, "He's here! He's here!" Amy shook her head, mortified at what Tony might think of her family.

The girls paused just outside the living room as Mr. Kashiwagi, retired for the evening with his coat and tie off, opened the door. Tony stood there, tall and handsome in surgeon's scrubs and white doctor's jacket, with a stethoscope hanging around his neck. "Trick or treat?" he grinned.

Amy took a deep breath and let it out slowly. Tony looked amazing.

Confused, Mr. Kashiwagi peered behind Tony to see if he had

come in a group. "Aren't you a little old to be trick-or-treating?"

Tony laughed nervously. He lifted the end of the stethoscope and raised his eyebrows like Groucho Marx. "Is the nurse ready?"

"I beg your pardon?" Mr. Kashiwagi replied, craning his neck.

"Better hurry," June said, shoving Amy forward, "before Dad slams the door on him."

"Sorry," Tony said, cutting his Groucho Marx impression short. "Is Amy—"

"I'm here," she said, stepping forward. She was followed by June, Kelly, and Mrs. Kashiwagi. Tony's eyes widened as he caught sight of her, and Mr. Kashiwagi turned to his daughter and stared at her, speechless, while Kelly flounced around in her pink tutu, begging to be noticed. "Mom, Dad, this is Tony Piccinin, and Tony, these are my sisters, June and Kelly."

Tony extended his hand to her father. "Mr. Kashiwagi, I shouldn't have assumed you'd know me. It's nice to meet you. My dad is Antonio Piccinin."

Mr. Kashiwagi ignored Tony's hand. Instead, he glared at his wife and spoke in rapid Japanese, as he always did when he was angry or did not want non-Japanese people to understand him. In this instance, it was both, as he raised his voice. "*Kono orokamono wa daredesu ka? Soshite, kare wa watashitachi no musume o hirotle nani o yatte iru?*"

Mrs. Kashiwagi replied, "*Watashi wa kare hakujindatta shirimasendeshita! Watashi wa, karera ga o mawashita tokiniha, hidzuke ni naru on nanoko ni ittaga, watashi wa kare ga amerikahito wa omoi mo shimasendeshita!*"

Covering for her boorish parents, June stepped in. "Where did you two meet?"

Tony lowered his hand. "Downstairs, in the store." He smiled nervously at Amy. "You look beautiful."

"Thank you. This was my mother's."

Tony cleared his throat, and her parents paused their arguing to get another look at him. He smiled. "Mrs. Kashiwagi, I see where Amy gets her good looks." But Amy's mother said nothing, a frozen expression on her face. Tony quickly added, "And her inner beauty." Finally, Amy's mother forced a smile.

While Amy covered her mouth and tried not to laugh, Tony lowered his eyes to her little sister. "And you, great costume! I bet you get a bunch of candy tonight." Kelly blushed and hid behind June's legs. He looked at Amy. "Are you ready?" The relief in his voice was palpable. Amy nodded and slipped past her father's firm stance.

"Be home early," her mother said. Amy shot her a look of understanding.

Smiling politely, Tony closed the door behind them. "Well, that was fun." Amy said, letting out a sigh of relief.

"Indeed." He chuckled as they passed some potted plants and walked down the hallway to the stairs. They continued to his father's car in silence until he said, "You don't speak Japanese, do you?"

"No, silly, I was born here. Do you know Italian?"

"*Tuo padre è una capra e un asino!*"

Amy laughed. "What does that mean?"

Tony had to think fast, as he had just called her father an old goat and an ass. "Um, a boy with a beautiful girl always sings," he laughed. "So Chattanooga Choo Choo, won't you choo choo me home?" he sang, ushering her into the car.

Amy giggled, sliding into the passenger seat and enjoying the butterflies in her stomach. They were only one minute into their date, and she was already having a good time. That is, until she glanced at her family's apartment and saw her father looking down on them with a scowl on his face.

* * * * *

Driving to the dance, Tony could not believe his good fortune. Amy looked so pretty, and she could not be nicer. And, apart from her dad, the family seemed like aces. He turned on the radio and cruised to a Cole Porter song, wondering what to say next. "So, uh, Amy—"

Unexpectedly, she grabbed his arm and yelled, "Stop!"

He managed to hit the brakes just as a stray dog wandered into the road, directly ahead. "You okay?" he asked, but she was already out of the car. He stepped out and watched as a big, rambunctious black lab licked her face.

Amy's worried face looked up at Tony. "We've got to get him home."

What? She had to be joking. They would be late to the dance, and besides, the dog could live anywhere. "He'll be fine," he said, checking his watch. "We're late."

"Look at him. He needs water, and his fur is all matted." She ran her hands over the animal's coat. "Oh, poor thing—"

Oh, great! An animal lover. Tony laughed to himself. "Are you sure?" Tony asked. "We don't know where he lives."

She examined the dog tag. "Do too. 1428 Elm."

"Elm Street is at least a mile away. What if nobody's home? Are we gonna wait there all night? On Hallowe'en?"

"We can be there in five minutes," Amy said, walking to the car. The lab followed her, panting all over the place.

It was no use. She had already let the dog into his father's car. Tony pictured his father seeing this hairy monstrosity in his precious automobile and cursing at the top of his lungs. He decided it would be okay, just this once. Besides, what his father did not know could not hurt him.

As Tony drove in the opposite direction of the dance, the dog slobbered all over the rear seats, creating a small puddle. Amy leaned over the bench seat and cooed, "Poor thing."

"Tell me about it," Tony mumbled. He made a mental note to clean that up later, or he would never be allowed to borrow the car again.

Ten minutes later, he pulled into 1428 Elm Street. His headlights illuminated a neglected two-story house in serious need of repair. "Well, it's haunted. That's perfect for tonight."

"Oh, stop," Amy said, getting out and heading up the path. She knocked on the front door, while Tony stayed back with the mutt and watched with curiosity. A man who had not seen a razor in weeks answered the door with a bowl of Hallowe'en candy in his hands. Tony could not hear what was said, but the gruff man wore an expression of disbelief. Finally, he followed Amy outside.

She opened the car door. "Tobias, come here," the gruff man said. But the dog whimpered and backed up. The man reached in, and Tony caught a strong whiff of cigarettes and alcohol. "C'mon, Tobias." The dog held its ground. "Don't make me come after you." He grabbed Tobias by the collar and yanked the cowering dog from the car. "Thanks," he said, to Tony, completely ignoring Amy. He walked the dog inside without another word.

Amy got back into the car. "I'm glad he got his dog back."

Tony pulled out of the driveway, and as he drove away, he stared at Amy, wondering if this was an isolated incident or if she was, in fact, a full-time do-gooder.

"What?" she asked, breaking his train of thought. "We had to help!"

He shook his head, a big grin on his face. Emilia would have never helped anyone in a million years, let alone a dirty, stray dog. This new girl was as down-to-earth as she was nutty, and he liked it that way.

Chapter 7

As the sounds of a wailing saxophone sliced through the walls of the school gymnasium, Tony gallantly opened the car door for Amy, offering his arm, and together, the doctor and the nurse entered the dance. The place was alive with orange and black streamers, balloons, and carved jack-o-lanterns. Witches, monsters, ghosts, and characters from *The Wizard of Oz* dotted the gym floor; even the chaperones were in costume. Tony waved to a few friends, who stared at him and his new girl. By now, the word of his temporary breakup with Emilia had spread.

Amy clung to Tony's arm as they approached the dance floor. He leaned into her ear, catching a light hint of her jasmine perfume. "Do you remember what I said about you being the second best dancer?"

She put a hand on his shoulder, flashing him a pretty white smile. "How could I ever forget something like that?" And as if on cue, the band struck the first few, unmistakable bars of Glenn Miller's 'In the Mood'.

Tony winked at her. "You're about to find out why." Pulling her in, he began the first steps of the East Coast Swing, and she caught on right away. She was a vibrant and energetic dancer, and she had her moves down pat. With those long legs and trim body, she matched him step for step as they gravitated toward the center of the crowded dance floor. The surrounding dancers moved aside to watch them, hooting and hollering for more as Tony and Amy cut a rug.

When the song ended there was a round of applause, and both of them caught their breath as they went in search of a refreshment. "You murdered it," he told her.

"That extra twist?" she asked.

"I like to improvise," he said, with a smile.

"Oh, yeah." Amy nodded her approval, and Tony poured two cups of punch. As they downed their drinks, the band struck up another song.

"Shall we?" he asked. Without hesitation, she put her hand in his, and they made their way back to the floor. Tony broke into the Jitterbug, and Amy joined him, moving to the music as fast as she could in her nurse's uniform. Three songs later, they could not take it anymore. They hustled off the dance floor, joining a few of Tony's teammates and their dates by the bleachers.

Paul pounded Tony on the shoulder. "Man, that was crazy. Where do you hide your bones when you do that?"

In their Hallowe'en costumes, everyone crowded around them. "Amy, these are my teammates, Bruno, our second baseman, and my sister Angela, Aldo and his date— uh— Emilia."

Well, this was awkward. Emilia had not taken the break-up well. Her green eyes burned into him, and Tony could not blame her for hating him when he called things off between them, asking for some space. After all, she had been looking forward to this dance for weeks. Her parents had commissioned an original fairy princess gown for this very occasion from a costumer at RKO Pictures. He tried not to let her presence bother him. After all, her parents were rich, she was young and beautiful, and besides, he knew Aldo had had a crush on her since freshman year. She would get over it.

Continuing the introductions, Tony said, "And you know Paul, our benchwarmer, and Isabella."

Paul scoffed, "Don't listen to him. He's our strikeout king. What do you see in this deuce anyway?"

"He's a deuce, all right." Amy said, putting a reassuring hand on Tony's back.

Anxious to finalize their after-party make-out plans, Tony said, "Guys, let's get these dolls something to drink." He and his buddies departed for the punch bowl, leaving Amy with the other girls.

* * * * *

As Emilia, Angela, and Isabella spoke amongst themselves, Amy pretended to be absorbed in the beautiful costumes on the dance floor, but Emilia's strident tones rang out, cutting through the music like a sharp blade. "Angela, why didn't you tell me she's a Jap? Wait 'til your mom finds out!"

Angela, dressed as Snow White, complete with cape and gown, apologized, "I didn't know. Really, I'm sorry. My brother never said anything, but once my mom knows, that'll be the end of her."

Amy's heart pounded from their insensitivity. What did she ever do to them? As much fun as she was having when they first arrived, now she just wanted to go home.

"And when that happens, he's coming back to me. You just watch," Emilia hissed.

Amy heard everything. *So, Tony and Emilia had been a couple!*

Emilia wheeled toward Amy and locked eyes with her. "You're nothing but a dirty little Jap girl."

"Excuse me?" Amy spluttered.

"C'mon, with ears that big, you heard me!" Emilia marched straight up to her and stared at the top of her head. "That's the ugliest thing I've ever seen," she spat, knocking Amy's nurse's cap right off.

Emilia whirled around and stormed off, closely followed by Isabella. But to Amy's horror, Angela came over and fumed, "Stay away from my brother! You hear me?"

Hot tears rose in Amy's eyes, but she would be damned if she would let those girls see them. Bending down, she picked up her cap. Feeling her hair for the stickpin, she realized it was missing, and immediately scanned the floor in a panic to find it. She rechecked her hair—nothing, the flooring again—nothing. She hated to do this, knowing how the girls would roar with laughter, but Amy got down on her hands and knees and searched through the confetti and streamers for her grandmother's stickpin. She had to find it!

Finally, Tony's shoes stop before her on the gym floor. "What're you doing?" he asked, squatting down.

She looked up at him helplessly, her eyes moist. "It's gone! My mom is gonna kill me."

"What's gone?" he asked, getting down on his hands and knees to join her.

"My grandmother's stickpin."

"What's that?"

"For my hair," she said, fighting back tears. "For holding up my hair!"

"What happened?" he asked, as he scoured through the decorations.

She was frantic. Her frustration was more than she could take. "I'll tell you what happened! Your ex had a hissy fit! She swung at me and knocked my hat off! Then her goon told me to stay away from you!"

"Her goon—"

"Your sister!" Amy wondered if he really was this stupid.

"I'm sorry," Tony said, rising to his feet. "This is all my fault." He held out his hand to help her up.

She got up and pulled out of his grasp. "Now, I'll never find it. It was the only thing of hers I had."

"I promise I'll find it. I'll ask everybody if they've seen it. I'll even check with the janitor on Monday."

She saw the sincerity in his eyes and his sad expression. He was not just some boy making empty promises. He was trying to right a wrong. She scanned the floor one last time, but it was futile.

"Let's get out of here," Tony said, giving her an apologetic look. "I promise I'll make it up to you."

Amy knew he was telling the truth. "Okay," she said, recovering her poise.

"Where would you like to go?" he asked, leading the way out.

"I know a soda shop by SC," she said, taking a hold of his hand to show Emilia and the other girls that she was unaffected.

"Swell. We'll go there." He smiled at her.

* * * * *

Tony wiped the chocolate milkshake off his lips and sank back into the red leather booth seats. With a smile on his face, he took in the moment—the prettiest nurse he had ever seen sat across from him, the joint was jumping with everyone in costume, and the music playing from the jukebox filled his soul.

"This is so much better than that crappy high school dance," he said. And it was. Without knowing it, they had crossed the demarcation line between high school and adulthood. "I wish there were more places like this."

"Yeah," Amy said. "Sometimes it's best to hang out where you don't hang out."

He pushed his empty glass away. "Yeah, I know what you mean. I like this crowd. And listen, I'm really sorry about what happened back there."

She sighed. "It's okay. I over-reacted."

"No, you didn't. And it's not okay."

"Thanks," Amy said. "But I'm fine now."

Just then, the jukebox clattered as another record slid on, this one a slow tune. "Want to?" he asked, touching her upturned palm.

She gazed into his eyes. "Sure, I'd like that."

He took her hand, and they squeezed between some couples on the dance floor and stood, pressed together. It was Hallowe'en, but it might as well have been Valentine's Day. Everywhere he looked, couples were kissing. She noticed it too. He could see her glancing over at them, until their eyes met. She blushed and looked away, then back to him.

The time felt right. Tony leaned in, hoping for the best, and as luck would have it, Amy leaned forward, too. Their lips made contact, and hers were soft, full, and intoxicating. The moment they kissed, he knew he wanted more—and not just physical intimacy. He wanted, had to have, more of her.

The song ended, and they floated off the dance floor, hand in hand. As they passed a booth full of rowdy guys, one of them called out, "Hey, Coke Boy!"

Tony paused, scanning for whoever said it, and found an annoying-looking clown staring back at him. He could not tell who it was behind the make-up, red nose, and wig, so he just ignored him and headed back to the booth.

"Coke Boy!" the clown said again. "You deaf or something?"

"Hi, Jeff," Amy said, frowning at the perpetrator. It took Tony a couple of seconds, then it came to him. The clown was Mr. Schultz's son from last Saturday's delivery run.

"Where's your Coke shirt?" Jeff asked, eliciting chuckles from his friends. "I thought you slept in it!"

Tony glared at him, his face burning hot. He felt that temper of his creeping up, but there was no way he was going to let it blow in front of Amy.

She tugged on his arm. "Let's go," she said, and he followed her lead.

As they left, Jeff bellowed, so that everyone could hear. "What does she taste like?" Half the joint heard him, and they quieted down to listen. "Let me guess, tuna fish!"

The place erupted into laughter, and Tony yanked his arm from Amy's grasp and stormed over to Jeff's table, getting into his face. "Get up!"

"What? Coke Boy can't take a joke?" Jeff scoffed.

Tony's face and neck turned bright red. "I said get up!" When Jeff just sat there with a shit-eating grin, Tony hauled him out of the booth by his shirt collar. As everyone watched, he loomed over Jeff with a fist over his face. "C'mon! Say something now, college boy!"

Jeff shrank back, stammering. "It— it was a joke. We were just joking. Right, boys?" His mates nodded in agreement.

Suddenly, Tony felt a small but strong hand on his arm, tugging, making him let go of Jeff. "Hey, he's not worth it. C'mon, let's go."

* * * * *

By the time they reached Kashiwagi's Korner Market, Tony had cooled down. Getting out of the car, Amy instinctively looked up. Tony followed her gaze to her father's silhouette standing at the window, peering down at them from behind the curtains. "Your dad?"

"Yeah, I'm late. I've got to go."

"I— I had a good time," Tony stuttered, suddenly embarrassed. "I'm so sorry about Emilia and what happened with Jeff. And don't worry, I'll talk to my sister."

She clutched his arm. "Please don't. If you don't react to her drama, it'll pass. Trust me, I've been there before."

He admired her strength of character. Letting something go without confrontation was definitely not in his repertoire. "You're something else, you know that?"

She smiled. "So are you." The lights in the Kashiwagi residence went out, and Amy's face soured. "I've really got to go." She opened the downstairs door. "I had a wonderful time."

And then she was gone.

Chapter 8

Amy opened the curtains wide, letting the morning sun shine on her face. She heard her youngest sister running down the hall, when her door burst open. Kelly leaped onto her bed in her pretty, white nightgown, and June followed, perching on the windowsill. "So tell us! C'mon, tell us what happened!"

Amy tried to be serene, but a rollercoaster of emotions flooded back to her. With Kelly in the room, she focused on the positive. "We talked. We danced." She started to glide around the room as if she was dancing with Tony again. "We held hands. We kissed. Everything was perfect."

"You kissed?" June asked, leaning forward, mouth wide open.

"Ew! You kissed a boy?" Kelly interrupted and made an ugly face, as she stood on the bed.

Amy mimicked Kelly's ugly face, then her dreamy look returned. "Yes, we were dancing, and I gave him the sign."

"What sign?" June asked.

Amy pretended that Tony held her. "I look up like this, close my eyes, and tilt my head like this, then he kisses me." When she reopened her eyes, she saw two amazed faces staring back at her.

"Wow!" June said. "I can't wait to go on a date."

Kelly scrunched up her face, pouted her lips, looked straight up, and closed her eyes. She looked so adorable that Amy planted a big wet one on her cheek.

"Yuck!" Kelly shouted, wiping off her face and bouncing on her sister's bed.

"Cooties. You got cooties," June teased.

* * * * *

As the Coca-Cola truck grounded to a halt in front of Grimaldi's Market, an antique shop next door caught Tony's eye. Mr. Piccinin turned off the engine. "Dad, can you handle this by yourself?"

His father followed his gaze. "Why, what's in there?"

"Nothing. I just have to buy something."

"Make it fast."

Tony bolted from the truck and called out a quick, "Thanks." He ran into the cramped store where a small, fastidious man stood behind a glass counter.

"May I help you?" the man asked, folding his immaculate hands.

Tony looked at all the beautiful ornaments, magnifying lenses, lamps, and furniture. Inside a glass case were a number of Asian fans, scrolls with neat lettering, and bamboo prints. "Do you have any Japanese stickpins?"

"Just one. It's over there." The clerk toddled over to another display case and polished the glass with a paisley handkerchief from his back pocket.

Peering in, Tony saw a beautiful stickpin with a floral design and ruby and pearl inlay. "I'll take it!" Instantly, he cursed himself for being so impulsive. "I mean, how much is it?"

The sales clerk meticulously took the stickpin out and laid it on a black velvet display board. "As an expert on exquisite Japanese stickpins, you know from the craftsmanship and intricate detail that this is one of the finest ever made."

Tony knew a hustle when he heard one, but he could not keep his dad waiting. He had to have it. Their next stop was Kashiwagi's Korner Market. "How much?" he asked again.

"Five dollars."

What? Where's the diamond? The most expensive stickpin should not have been more than a dollar seventy-five or two bucks, tops. It was all he had on him. He pulled out five one-dollar bills and held them for a moment. He had to make it right with Amy. "Here," he said, giving the money to the clerk.

The man delicately put the stickpin in a paper pouch for safekeeping and handed it to Tony. "Thank you, young man. You have a marvelous day."

"Yeah, yeah," Tony muttered, as he ran out of the shop.

When he reached the truck, his father was already behind the wheel. "Did you find what you were looking for?"

"Not exactly." There was no need for his dad to know his business.

His father looked at his watch. "We're behind. Let's— what is it you kids say?"

"Skiddle." Tony chuckled, putting him in a better mood.

His dad put the truck into gear. "Let's skedaddle."

Tony laughed. "Dad, you have to get with the times. It's *skiddle*."

* * * * *

On a Saturday morning, with no football game or activities on campus, the store was as dead as a raft in the middle of a calm ocean. Amy was practically dozing off to the strains of Jimmy Dorsey's 'Green Eyes' when she heard the Coca-Cola truck pull up. Immediately, she popped up, fixed her hair, fluffed out her skirt, and leaned on the counter as if she had nothing better to do than count the packs of gum next to the cash register.

The cowbell clanged, and she tried to be cool as she looked up. "Oh, good morning, Mr. Piccinin," she said, glancing at Tony with a subdued smile.

"Good morning, Amy," Mr. Piccinin replied.

Tony set down the loaded dolly. "Hi."

"Hi," she said, as if he were merely the delivery boy and not the dashing beau who had swept her off her feet last night.

"Mr. Piccinin, my father said he wants to talk to you as soon as you came in. He's in his office."

"Oh? Okay. Thank you. Tony, can you handle things?"

"I got it, Dad," Tony shot Amy a full-out grin behind his father's back as he walked to Mr. Kashiwagi's office.

She watched as Tony refilled the shelves with Coca-Cola bottles. He looked so smooth in his short-sleeved, delivery shirt, which showed off his bulging biceps. She was not sure if she should tell him in case he had changed his mind about her, but she risked it. "I had a great time last night."

Tony gave her a pensive expression, and Amy thought he was going to break it off with her. "Me too," he said instead. Then he reached into his breast pocket. "I have something for you." He produced a small envelope, which he tilted into his open palm. A beautiful ruby and pearl stickpin fell into his hand. "I'll find the one that's lost. I just want you to have this one for now."

"Oh, Tony, it's lovely," she gasped, throwing her arms around him.

He felt her body quivering, and though his father could return at any moment, he held on. He was in uncharted territory. Emilia had never responded like this to any of his presents, and he did not know what to do or say. When she finally pulled away, he stammered, "Are you f— free on Friday?"

"What, no whistle?" she joked. They laughed, then separated to a safe distance as they heard his father's footsteps on the wooden floor.

Folding his papers, Mr. Piccinin walked toward the doorway. "Amy, take care. Romeo, the dolly."

I hope her father put in a good word for me. Tony shrugged his shoulders, raised his eyebrows, and mouthed the word "Romeo" to Amy. He grabbed the two-wheeler and looked back, waiting for her answer.

"Yes," she said.

"Till then, my Juliet," he said as the door closed.

* * * * *

As they drove away, Tony stared out the truck window and thought about next Friday night—where could they go, what could they do, and especially, what it would be like to kiss her again. After settling in, Mr. Piccinin broke the silence, "That Amy sure is cute. And she has tons of personality. I want you to know that I have nothing against you two." Tony did not want to jinx it by saying anything, so he just nodded. But as they stopped at a red light, his father's face took on a worried, serious expression that made Tony's stomach clench. "But Mr. Kashiwagi told me you aren't to see her again."

Tony's heart-beat rose to a panic. "Why? What's wrong?"

"I don't know. But he's her father, and what he says goes!"

Tony started to protest, but his father shot him a look that defied argument.

* * * * *

Without knocking, Maria Piccinin entered the boys' bedroom. She was on the warpath; that much was clear. Marco, getting a head start on his algebra homework, tried to cut her off at the pass. "Is Dad ready?"

"I don't know!" she snapped, stopping in front of Tony, who was lounging on his bed. He braced for what he knew was coming. "Why didn't you take Emilia to the dance?"

He tried to be nonchalant. "She isn't my type. I've been thinking—"

"Sit up!" she demanded, and Tony did as he was told. "What do you mean she's not your type? You've dated for a year!"

"Mom, she just isn't for me. She's self-centered and doesn't know anything about sports." As soon as the words were out of his mouth, he knew he should not have called her self-centered. *Dammit! Keep your mouth shut!*

His mother threw her hands up in the air in frustration. "She's not self-centered, and you know it! And for Christ's sake, you can talk to your brother about sports! You have to realize, you can't have everything in a wife." She paused. "Who did you take?"

He fought the urge to tell her, but he was trapped. "Her name's Amy. You'd like—"

"Don't tell me who I would and wouldn't like! And aren't you forgetting something?" Her eyes narrowed, then she really exploded. "She's a Jap! Everyone's been calling me! You're not to see her again! Do you understand me?"

"But Mom, you're overreacting. You always say don't judge a book by its cover. Her skin color is just her cover. She's terrific. Just ask Dad. He'll tell—"

"I'm telling you!" She drew closer to him, her eyes mere inches from his. "You're not to see her again! Do I make myself clear?"

"Mom, I'm eighteen," Tony said, pushing his fears aside in frustration. "I can choose my own girlfriend!"

Her face got red, and Tony swore he could see steam shooting out of her ears. He had not seen her this angry since he and Paul got sick on that pint of whiskey last year. "Like hell you will, or you'll be out of a home!"

Right then, Paul walked into the room, carrying his baseball spikes and glove. "Hey, Mrs. P," he said.

"It's Mrs. Piccinin to you and your friends!" She shoved a finger in Paul's face. "Look at me when I'm talking to you! You put him up to it! You'd better fix the damage you've caused." With that, Tony's mother stormed out of the room.

Paul waited for her to be out of earshot. "What is she yapping about this time?"

Tony rifled one of Marco's comics at his head, but he ducked. It hit the closet door behind him. "Guess, you moron. I knew she'd go ballistic. And get this. Amy's father doesn't want me to see her either. I can't win."

"They're putting the screws to you," Paul said. "That's what they're doing."

"That's what they think," Tony said. He was not going to let his parents or hers control him. "We already have a date for Friday."

Marco got up from his desk. "What? Tony, that's not a good idea, and you know it. You should give up. You know you can't win."

Paul sneered at Marco. "Tony, I never knew you had three sisters."

Tony nodded toward his brother. "Yeah, that one just got her first period."

"Hey, guess what." Paul announced, smugly. "That new girl— you know— her locker is by Mr. Warner's room. I made out with her last night."

"You're out of your mind," Tony retorted.

"Listen. After you left, I asked Isabella where you went. She told me the whole story, and I kicked her to the curb right there. Right there in the gym, I let her have it. Well, when I was done, the new girl was just standing there, so I asked her to dance. After a few dances we went to Burke's for a soda, then we made out."

"What's her name?" Marco asked.

"Here's the funny part, Champ," Paul said, putting his arm around Marco's shoulder. "I'm sure she told me because she called me Paul several times, but I have no idea! Not even a clue!"

A moment later, Tony's father appeared at the door, wearing a New York Yankees cap and holding a baseball glove. "You boys ready? Let's skiddle."

"I'm up," Marco said, grabbing his glove.

One by one, they passed Mr. Piccinin in the doorway. "That's impressive, Mr. P," Paul said.

"Don't encourage him," Marco said, bolting past his smiling father.

Chapter 9

Tony patted his neck with a tad of cologne, but not too much. He had told his folks he was going to the movies with Paul and did not want either of them getting suspicious when he left the house smelling of Old Spice. He had a great night planned. Humphrey Bogart, his favorite actor, was starring in a new picture, *The Maltese Falcon*, and he was anxious to see it with Amy. Emilia would have balked because the crime drama would be too hard to follow. Afterwards, they would go to a soda shop for a milkshake.

He dashed up the stairs to the Kashiwagis' apartment, his heart halfway up his throat, praying Amy's father had reconsidered his position. *My God, it's 1941, not 1911. What is it with these old people?*

He knocked, and the door opened a split-second later, as if someone had been expecting him. But it was the wrong person. Mr. Kashiwagi stood there, cold and stern, with Amy behind him. Tony extended his hand. "Mr. Kashiwagi, it's nice to see you again."

Amy's father took a long, hard look at his hand then raised his head, which had turned reddish-brown. "I told your father you're not to come here! Didn't he tell you? Or don't you respect him? Or me?" As he continued his barrage of complaints, Amy diverted her eyes to something in the hallway.

"Yes, yes," Tony stammered. "Of course I respect you, and my father, too. I just wanted to—"

Mr. Kashiwagi cut him off. "If you ever see my daughter again, I'll buy my cola elsewhere. Am I clear?" He slammed the door in Tony's face.

Tony fell against the hallway wall, dropping into a squat, pulling on his hair, not knowing what to do. From the ceramic pot next to him, a piece of white paper flashed. He slid it out and read it: *SC Library, Sunday at 3, Amy.* A slow smile crept onto Tony's face. Maybe there was hope yet.

He slipped the note into his pocket, replacing it with a stickpin he had found at a flea market after school.

* * * * *

Amy clutched her biology book to her chest and poked her head into the kitchen. "Mom," she said, holding up her textbook for emphasis, wondering if she was overdoing it, "I'm going to the library."

From the counter, Mrs. Kashiwagi paused and looked at her, dish towel in hand. Was she noticing how nicely her hair was done, or the fact that she was wearing some make-up? Amy felt guilty, but her mother did not seem to spot anything out of the ordinary. And if she did, she was not showing it. "Okay, sweetheart," she said, wiping the kitchen counter.

"See you later," Amy said, rushing out the door and down the stairs. She crossed the street onto the University of Southern California campus, with its green lawns and palm trees, checking her watch anxiously. Three o'clock. She was late. Rushing to the library, nerves on high alert over the possibility of her father seeing her from the store, she approached the building's steps, hoping for the best. One scan of the majestic steps, and she spotted him.

Tony, at the top of the stairs, wore a madras shirt and blue jeans. He smiled when he saw her—out of relief, it seemed. Amy returned the smile and raced up the steps. They kissed quickly, sweetly, without hesitation or fanfare. Then, he held out his hand. In his palm lay another stickpin. This one was decorated with bamboo trees against a background of mother-of-pearl. "No, I can't," she protested, gently pushing his hand away. "This is the third one! It's costing you a small fortune."

He opened her palm and placed it inside. "It's the least I can do until I find the one that's lost. Amy, please take it. I want you to have it."

"Oh, Tony, you don't know how much this means to me." She took it and sighed, appreciating his thoughtful gift. She gave him her books to hold, then twisting her hair up she slid the pin into place. "Thank you so much."

"It looks perfect on you."

Abandoning the library, Tony and Amy saw *The Maltese Falcon* on their first illicit date. It would become their favorite movie. Afterwards, they drove to the coast. Tony rolled up his jeans, and they played tag in their bare feet, relishing the feeling of the sand between their toes. When it was Tony's turn to run, he ran backwards to make it easier for her, and when she caught him, they fell into the sand. She kissed him for the third time. Then, he kissed her for the fourth time. Soon, they lost count.

The next weekend, they studied and went to the Trojan Inn for a hamburger and chocolate malt. The weekend after that, they rode bicycles. At some point, Tony took her to see *Suspicion*, starring Cary Grant and Joan Fontaine. As they left the theater, Tony did his Cary Grant impression. "There's only one dame prettier and more charming than Joan Fontaine."

"Who?" she asked, playing along.

"Darling," he cracked, still in his Cary Grant voice. "You have to guess?"

Amy slid her arm through his. "Honey, can you give me a tiny, itty-bitty clue? Please?"

"She wears a red polka-dot dress." Amy looked down, and Tony switched his voice to imitate a Hollywood narrator. "The beautiful starlet looks down at her dress. She points to herself quizzically. Cary nods. She throws her arms around him, and they—"

Before he could finish, Amy locked his lips in a feverish kiss, laughing, wishing she could take this moment, frame it, and make it last forever.

* * * * *

Mr. Kashiwagi left his store in Hollywood and headed back home to check his ledger again. His inventory numbers were wrong, and if he did not figure out the problem soon, he would never sleep that night. Driving down Van Ness Avenue, he passed the new Melvan Theater on the corner of Melrose Avenue. He looked over and saw a couple kissing. *Damn kids and their disgusting displays of affection! If they have to kiss, they should do it indoors where no one has to see them.*

Then, in his rearview mirror, he noticed the red polka-dot dress, the jet black hair, the waist, those legs, and the slender arms lovingly draped around the boy's neck. He would know her anywhere. And worse—he would know that dago anywhere. At the corner, he slammed on the brakes, narrowly missing a black woman crossing the street who cursed at him. He made a quick right turn and stepped on it. Then, he made another right and another right. Circling the block, he looked for his daughter, but she and that boy were gone.

Chapter 10

When Tony got home, he found his parents sitting at the kitchen table in the dark. "Hey, who died?" he joked, opening the ice box for a bottle of milk. His dad looked at him with a grave expression. Then he noticed the redness in his mother's eyes. "Is Grandpa okay?" he asked, feeling nauseous all of a sudden.

Mr. Piccinin shook his head. His fists were clenched. "You wouldn't listen, would you? You just had to push it!"

"Push what?" Tony asked, even though he now knew what they were talking about. It had been only a matter of time before his parents found out he was still seeing Amy. He did not understand why it was such a big issue with them. Hell, his father was divorced or annulled, whatever people called it, when his mother married him.

His mother began to cry. "How are we going to pay the bills, Tony? We have to eat."

Tony cocked his head to one side. "Will someone please tell me—"

"Are *you* going to pay the bills?" Maria hissed. "Huh? After all, you're the one who got us in this mess!"

Clearly, this was not about Amy but something much worse. Tony looked at his father and hoped for more sense out of him. "What mess? What is Mom talking about?"

His father's face was flustered and red. "You know damn well what you did. You've got three seconds to tell us."

Tony's mouth hung open, as he scoured his memory. "Unless

you're talking about—" He trailed off, not wanting to mention Amy in case he was mistaken.

With a darkness in his eyes, which Tony had never seen before, his father rose out of his chair. "Mr. Kashiwagi saw the two of you today. He cancelled our account. I've never been more disappointed in you."

Tony watched helplessly as his mother laid her head on the table and sobbed. "It's all gone. Everything we worked so hard for."

Tony's body felt as if the earth had moved out from under him. He leaned against the counter for support. "Mom, Dad, I'm so sorry. I just—" He wanted to say how much he loved Amy and how much she made him feel loved, more than Emilia ever could, but now the stupidity of what he had done, his blatant disregard slapped him hard.

You just—," his father flared. "You just don't think rules apply to you! Do you?"

Desperate, Tony went to his father's side and grabbed his hands. "Let me help! Please! I promise! I'll find us some new accounts."

His father pulled his hands away. "You think it's easy getting clients? Well, it's not!"

His mother looked up, dabbing at her tears with a napkin. "I told you to leave her alone. Why didn't you listen?"

Tony heard the bedroom doors popping open down the hall. "I can't just leave her alone," he snapped. "That's what you don't understand. I love her!"

The words sent his mother into a fit, and she exploded. "No you don't! No son of mine is marrying a yellow skin!"

"Mom, you can't possibly mean that."

"Don't think I don't!" she yelled.

Enough was enough. Tony spun around, ready to storm out of the room. His parents were just like everyone else—judgmental and closed-minded. Why could they not see that it did not matter what color anybody's skin was?

"Don't walk away from your mother while she's talking to

you," his father said in a tone so chilling that Tony did not dare take another step.

He stopped and looked at his parents. "How can I make you understand? Emilia never cared about me. Amy does. She knows me better than Emilia ever could. Don't you want that for me?"

Mr. Piccinin's pain was evident in his eyes. He had said he did not mind. Why was he changing his tune now? Was it the money? But his father just turned away and walked towards the living room.

"Dad, you understand what I'm saying, don't you?" His father paused for a second. For a split second, Tony hoped he might turn around and apologize, take him in his arms, and tell him everything would be okay, but he continued to walk away.

* * * * *

Tossing and turning, sleep evaded him that night. Tony stared at the ceiling. At one point he threw a framed photo of Emilia across the room, shattering the glass and scaring the bejeezus out of Marco.

What had he done? Or rather, what had Mr. Kashiwagi done? Was this the price he had to pay for loving his daughter? He had never thought it possible that Mr. Kashiwagi would sour a business deal just because he was dating Amy. What was so wrong about that? Would he prefer some Japanese Joe who would chisel her? He might not be the brightest crayon in the tin box, but he was solid. He would treat her right! Exactly what he would want from his own son-in-law if he ever had a daughter.

But worse, his family was now in financial jeopardy because of him. His dad had worked hard to make every customer happy, putting in long hours to provide for his family. There was not a thing he would not do for his clients. Hell, every Christmas he delivered a large box of Italian candy to all his accounts to thank them for their business, and he used his own money.

The more Tony thought about the unfairness of it all and how he had failed his father, the more he knew that no matter what it took, he had to make things right again.

* * * * *

On Monday, right after school, Tony took the city bus to Kashiwagi's Korner Market. Amy was not behind the counter; instead a blond girl he had never seen before was under the watchful eye of Mrs. Kashiwagi. "Hello, can I help you?" she asked, eager to please. "I'm new here, but I'm learning fast! What are you looking for? My name's Debbie by the way!" Finally she paused for a breath, noticing for the first time Mrs. Kashiwagi's hardened expression toward the young man.

"I'm looking for Mr. Kashiwagi," Tony replied, smiling despite his dark mood.

"He's in his office," Debbie said, then she was hushed by a firm hand on her shoulder. Mrs. Kashiwagi did not speak, nor did she try to stop Tony as he blew past them and hammered on the office door. The door did not open. But Mr. Kashiwagi had to come out sometime, and Tony was prepared to wait there until he did.

After an hour, Mr. Kashiwagi emerged from his office. He stopped short when he saw Tony standing there. "You listen to me," he said. "When I tell you not to see my daughter, you are *never* to see her again. You understand?" His cold eyes bored holes in Tony's heart.

"Yes, sir, it's just that—"

"It's just nothing." Mr. Kashiwagi cut him off. "And there is *nothing* you can do for your father. I've already made arrangements with Royal Crown Cola for my stores. Now leave." Tony held his gaze for a long time, but Mr. Kashiwagi did not relent. As he slunk out, Tony could not help but notice the helpless look on Mrs. Kashiwagi's face.

To rectify the situation, Tony had to replace the lost business. The Kashiwagi account covered five stores, so he needed to get five new accounts to cover the deficit. His dad was right. This was going to be tough, but he had to make it work. He either had to call on brand new stores that did not have a soda account yet, or call on existing stores that were carrying a competitor's brand and replace it with Coca-Cola.

Yet after hitting the pavement all week, he had gotten nowhere.

Chapter 11

On Sunday, Tony attended early Mass. After church, he changed into his Coca-Cola work shirt and cap, drove the family car across town, and pulled up at the first grocery store on the list, Galco's Old World Grocery. It was 9:10 a.m. Taking a deep breath in the cool air, he put on his most charming smile and walked through the door. "Good morning," he said to the owner who was going over some receipts behind the counter. "I'd like to talk to you about your cola needs."

"Now?" said the man, as he lit a cigarette. He seemed irritated, but Tony had learned from his dad that there was never a good time for a sales call; he had to make the most of it while he had their attention. "I'm a bit tired, kid."

"Sir, that's what Coca-Cola is for. A little pick me up when you need it the most." Tony popped open two cold bottles of Coca-Cola and handed one to the owner.

The owner took a drink. He might be tired, but he was not too tired to drink a free soda. "I admit that hits the spot, but I'm a RC man myself. Sorry kid." He turned back to his receipts.

Hmm. Tony detected some interest, but it was too early in his presentation to knock the competition; a tactic he had tried in previous calls to no prevail. Now, he had a novel idea. He smiled and tapped the owner on the shoulder. "Yes, Royal Crown is a terrific product." He took a long slug from his bottle and sighed. "But I'm a Coke man, myself."

The owner smiled, amused with Tony's efforts. "So what can

you offer me that my RC guys don't?"

"I'm not looking to replace anything, sir. I just want to give your customers the choice they're looking for. You're an RC man; I'm a Coke man. Why not carry both and get everyone's business?" Tony smiled.

The owner nodded, impressed. "And how do you aim to do that?"

Tony looked at the RC display. It was half-empty. "How often does your RC guy deliver?"

"Once a week, if I'm lucky."

Tony saw his opening and took it. It was just like pitching. Once he knew the batter's weakness, striking him out was only a matter of time. "My dad usually delivers twice a week. But for you, he'll swing by three times a week, just to make you happy."

The owner tried to hide his surprise, but when he saw Tony's earnestness, he could not help the big, fat smile that spread across his face. "C'mon, three times a week? Really? Who's your dad?"

"Antonio Piccinin. He's been with Coke for twenty years. He hasn't lost a customer yet, and he doesn't aim to." Tony had not intended to lie, but then again, he had not. Technically, his dad had not lost the Kashiwagi account. He had.

The owner sat up a little straighter. "I've heard of your dad." He scratched the stubble on his chin. "He's got a good reputation."

"Exactly! You can't lose." Tony stood, stiffly, proudly, afraid to express any more emotion than he already had. This was the adult world, a world of secret negotiations and back room deals. A world he had no clue about. But he knew that people only wanted one thing— what they wanted when they wanted it.

The owner looked at him, crossing his arms. "I do if you don't show.'"

Tony nodded. He figured the owner was marking his territory, letting him know who was boss. "I understand. But don't worry, he'll be here."

The man thought some more, nodded, and made a few

calculations on the back of a receipt with a pencil. Then he looked up. "What the heck, I'll give you three months to prove yourself." He extended his hand, and Tony took it in a firm grasp, just like his father had taught him, and shook it.

"Thank you, sir. You won't regret it."

* * * * *

Antonio rose from his bed; sunlight crept through the shades. His delivery uniform was washed and pressed, hanging on the closet door, as always. He felt anxious, like he was late for work, but it was Sunday. Slowly, he stretched and walked into the kitchen, where Maria stood washing dishes.

The two of them had weathered many storms together, and this was just another setback. They would get through it like they had gotten through everything else. He worked hard to provide for her and the kids, but they were so close to the margin that one account, one measly account, could throw the whole family into a tailspin. He was just going to have to work harder. He had already added a small account that week. It might take some time, but eventually he would replace the Kashiwagi business.

Maria had an uncanny ability to hear him no matter how quietly he padded down the hallway. "Coffee's on the table. Tony left a note. It's there on the table."

He lifted the scrap of paper: *I'll be back by 3. Tony.* "Where did he go?"

"I don't know, but if he didn't go to Mass, he's in trouble." Then, Mrs. Piccinin's voice turned melancholy. "Do you remember what today is?"

He racked his brain. *What is it? Can it be their anniversary? No. That's in July. One of the children's birthdays? No, they're all done for the year.* "Sure, I do," Mr. Piccinin said, buying himself a few extra seconds. He scanned the calendar on the refrigerator as his wife continued washing dishes. The 7th had a big red circle around it. He went to her and hugged her from behind. "Your mother's birthday."

She trembled. "I always wish she could've seen the kids, Antonio. She always wanted to be a grandmother."

He eased his wife around until they were face to face. "She can see the kids," he reassured her.

She fell into his arms and cried.

* * * * *

It had turned out to be a beautiful Los Angeles day—brilliant blue skies and a refreshing breeze. With the car windows down, Tony grabbed his list and uncapped a pen. At Patterson's Country Market, he marked an X next to it. He looked at the list: six X's stood out in marked contrast to the three check marks he had put next to Fullerton's General Store, Matheson's Meat Mart, and Galco's Old World Grocery. But he smiled nonetheless. Three out of nine was not bad, and he was plugging up the hole he had lanced through his family's financial situation. But before he called it a day, he wanted one more.

Tony cranked the engine and headed a little farther into town, to the last three stores on his list. Big band music played on the car radio. It was something new and unfamiliar, and Tony turned it up. He could not wait to give his family the good news when he got home. He tapped his fingers on the steering wheel, thinking of Amy. He had thought of her so much this past week; his heart ached.

Without warning, the music shut off abruptly. Tony heard a cough, followed by the station announcer's voice: "We interrupt this program to bring you breaking news. Early this morning, Japanese fighter planes bombed Pearl Harbor, Hawaii. An unidentified number are injured and dead. Stay tuned for further updates."

What? An attack? What does this mean? Are we at war? Immediately, Tony made a U-turn, screeching his father's tires and leaving tire marks on the road, and sped home as fast as he could.

Chapter 12

As Amy paced fretfully up and down the length of her bedroom, her fingers toyed with one of Tony's precious stickpins, turning it over and over in her hand. Every time she heard traffic on the road outside, she peered out the window in hope of seeing the Piccinin family car. But Tony never drove by.

In the living room, Kelly practiced 'Silent Night' on the piano. Her recital was in five days, and Amy's patience was wearing thin. If she heard that song just one more time, she knew she would go crazy.

"Amy, keep Kelly quiet!" her father called. "The President is about to speak."

Amy joined her family in the living room, where they had gathered around the radio. Her father, stiff and formal as ever, looked haggard, and her mother clung to his shoulder. Kelly continued playing, too young to understand the events spiraling outside their four walls. But Amy knew. Somehow, she could tell that everything was about to change, that things were in fact already changing, and not just between her and Tony.

"Kelly, Kelly, stop playing for a minute," Amy said, but her little sister insisted on finishing the song.

The unmistakable tones of President Roosevelt's voice came on the radio, and her father turned the volume up. "Shhh!" Amy hissed to Kelly, joining her on the piano bench. At long last the determined pianist quit playing, surprised by the urgency in her sister's warning. "Sorry, but we need to hear the President." Sensing her family's unease,

Kelly reached for Amy's hand and held it tightly.

The President cleared his throat then began his address. *"Mr. Vice President, Mr. Speaker, Members of the Senate, and of the House of Representatives: Yesterday, December 7th, 1941—a date which will live in infamy—the United States of America was suddenly and deliberately attacked by naval and air forces of the Empire of Japan."*

Many more words followed, but Amy found it hard to focus. The end of the President's speech chilled her to her very soul. *"With confidence in our armed forces, with the unbounding determination of our people, we will gain the inevitable triumph—so help us God. I ask that the Congress declare that since the unprovoked and dastardly attack by Japan on Sunday, December 7th, a state of war has existed between the United States and the Japanese empire."*

Mr. Kashiwagi stood and abruptly switched the radio off. Amy had never seen such desolation in his eyes before. Her father sat back down, putting his head in his hands, the first sign of weakness he had ever shown in front of his children. Then, as if realizing this, he suddenly sat up straight and composed. The girls shot each other tentative looks, and then all eyes returned to him. Amy wanted him to speak, to stand, to lecture them, order them around, or just give them something to do. Instead, he sat in stoic silence.

"Daddy, is everything okay?" Kelly asked quietly.

Her father looked over at his daughter. Then, without replying, he stood and retreated to his room.

* * * * *

Tony stared at his corn flakes. He and his dad were dressed for work when the kitchen door opened. Marco carried his newspaper satchel. "Did everyone get a paper?" his mother asked.

"Yes," Marco said, winking at his brother and placing his last paper on the table.

But Tony did not react. Instead, he read the headlines—more talk on the Pearl Harbor attack. He peeled off the front section. "Dad," he grunted, handing his father the rest of the newspaper. They were finally speaking again, but not exactly communicating.

His father crunched on his cereal and glanced at his son. "No sports?" His tone suggested he did not expect an answer.

Tony shook his head and gave him one anyway. "The war."

His parents looked at each other with concern. This was happening quite frequently these days, these silent exchanges, but Tony ignored it. He had never been much interested in politics, or government, to say nothing of foreign governments, but now he could not get enough. Every day, he read the paper thoroughly and listened to the radio for the latest developments. It was all happening so fast, like a broken dam. First it was Pearl Harbor, followed by the President's speech, and then Germany and his beloved Italy declared war on the United States.

Tony scanned the front page until he saw it. He read it quickly, clearing his throat to get his father's attention. When that did not work, he turned to face him. "Dad, doesn't Mr. Kashiwagi own a store on Terminal Island?"

The island was a Japanese fishing community off the coast of Los Angeles, where the men fished the Pacific waters of Southern California while their wives and daughters worked in the canneries, cleaning and packaging the fish they had caught.

"Yes," his father said, giving him a disinterested look.

"Dad, listen to this!" Tony read aloud from the newspaper. "All Japanese homes, businesses, and fishing boats on Terminal Island must be evacuated by nine tonight by order of the United States Army."

The Army believed an attack on the West Coast was imminent, and that the Japanese community on the island would aid or abet the enemy even though there was no evidence to support such an allegation.

Tony paused and studied his father before speaking, then asked, "Dad, can you do the route by yourself today?"

His father narrowed his eyes at him. Surely, he was remembering all of the trouble he had caused him. "Why?" he asked.

"I'll borrow Grandpa's truck and help Mr. Kashiwagi clear out the store. Even if he says no, I should at least offer. Shouldn't I?" Tony paused. "That should go a long way to making amends."

His parents looked at each other, but before his mother could weigh in, his father spoke, his first sign of interest in anything Tony had said all morning. "Go ahead."

His mother was unable to control her feelings. She pounded her fist against the counter, and sputtered, "But we're at war with those people!" Tony and Marco met each other's gaze. Their mother could run the household and the kids' lives as she saw fit, but this outburst—an act of defiance against her husband—was a first.

Tony lingered a while, just to watch and see how his father would handle the situation, and the girls quickly came out of their bedroom to see what all the racket was about.

* * * * *

Accompanied by Marco, Tony drove Grandpa's truck in absolute silence. They had never seen their parents fight like that before. While their father was the quiet type, he demanded respect, and while their mom might voice her opinion or raise her concerns now and again, she had never once questioned one of her husband's decisions. The shouting and yelling that ensued was something they would never forget.

By the time he and his brother got off the bridge at Terminal Island, half of Los Angeles appeared to have descended there in force. Trucks and automobiles were double-parked on both sides of the road, obstructing traffic, and crowds of people hustled past, shouting. Tension suffocated the air. The boys sat to attention, their eyes glued to the windshield.

"I wasn't expecting this," Tony said, staring at the chaos before them.

Marco's voice was somber. "I know. Now we'll never get out of here."

But Tony was not talking about the traffic. He was talking

about all the Japanese people who were being forced out. Where would they go?

Without directions, they drove around as best as they could until they found Kashiwagi's Fish & Food Market. Somehow they managed to find a tiny parking spot on the crowded street just down from the store, next to the docks. Honks from impatient drivers sounded from behind them as Tony managed to angle into the space, then back out, and then back in. The truck was only just far enough out of traffic to avoid being clipped.

As they got out of the pick-up, Tony felt his stomach rising into his chest. Would Mr. Kashiwagi be there? Would he be furious and demand he leave at once? No matter what happened, Tony resolved to try and help.

Reaching the end of the docks, Tony and Marco approached a Japanese fisherman and a white businessman deep in discussion. "Sorry pal," the white man said, with a wad of cash in his hand and a staid look on his face.

"But I have five thousand dollars in this boat!" the fisherman protested.

The businessman did not appear to be malicious, more like a man looking after his family, just like his own father. "I'm sure you do, but three hundred is the best I can do in today's market. Surely, you understand?"

As Tony and Marco passed by, the fisherman shook his head, close to tears, and Tony muttered loud enough so that the guy with the money could hear, "What a crumb."

The opportunist looked up at Tony, a flash of indignation on his face, and then went back to counting out twenty-dollar bills into the fisherman's trembling hands.

They stepped into Mr. Kashiwagi's store and found a beehive of activity, with everything at deep, discounted prices. Mr. Kashiwagi spotted Tony as soon as he and Marco walked in. If he was irritated at their last encounter, now he was downright livid. "What do you want?" he yelled. "Didn't I tell you never to come around us again?"

Suddenly, Tony second-guessed his decision to come here in the middle of a stressful situation. He could not speak.

"Well? Out with it!" Mr. Kashiwagi demanded.

"I— I— Dad thought we should help if you need us. We— we've got a truck." Tony shoved his thumb behind him to indicate that they had a vehicle that would help him clear out.

Mr. Kashiwagi looked both angry and stunned. He stood there, searching for the right words, and Tony thought he would be at the receiving end of another tongue lashing when an employee came in from the back room, carrying a stack of packing cartons in his hands. Mr. Kashiwagi stopped him and said, *"Anata ga koko ni korera no bokkusu o doroppo suru koto ga dekimasu. Korera wa tasukete iru."* The worker nodded and dumped the boxes at Tony and Marco's feet. "Well? Don't just stand there. Get to work!"

Chapter 13

After spending the day clearing out Kashiwagi's Fish & Food Market, Tony drove the truck, loaded down like a pack mule, to Mr. Kashiwagi's store on Jefferson Boulevard. Boxes blocked his rearview mirror, and sacks of potatoes, carrots, and celery, which hung over the truck bed, obstructed his side mirrors. At every turn, Tony and Marco expected the pick-up to topple, but somehow they made it.

"We good on your side?" Tony asked Marco, who nodded yes.

At Kashiwagi's Korner Market, Tony jolted to a stop behind a sedan laden down with suitcases and boxes. A husband and a wife, both Japanese, eyed the truck as they got out. In the backseat of their car, a little girl and boy smeared their noses against the window and wagged their fingers from behind their ears.

"Charming," Tony grunted. He slung a forty-pound sack of carrots over his shoulder and grabbed two bags of potatoes with his free hand. "Come on," he told his brother.

The cowbell clanged. It was the sweetest sound he had heard in a long time. As he and Marco walked in, Amy looked up from behind the counter, her face lighting up like a Christmas tree. Right away, his heart felt at ease. "Tony!" she shrieked, racing to him. "Put those down. Thank you! Thank you!" Tony dropped the bags, and she barreled into him, flinging her arms around him. He melted into her warmth and closed his eyes. They kissed.

"God, I've missed you," Tony whispered, feeling her heart thumping against his chest. His whole body longed for her.

"Hey!" Marco coughed, dropping his load onto the floor with a loud thump. "No canoodling."

They broke their embrace, and Amy surveyed the younger boy with interest. "Marco, I bet." She hugged him. "Thank you for helping my dad out."

"What, no kiss?" he joked, reaching out and fake-punching her on the arm.

Startled, a horrified expression crossed Amy's pretty features, as she looked to Tony for help.

"He's pulling your leg," he said.

"Oh!" She smiled with relief.

"Watch this," Marco said, imitating Amy's terrified reaction, and to his delight, she roared with laughter.

Amy held her arms out wide and said, "Fine, come here, you." She hugged Marco again, and this time, she kissed him on the cheek.

Tony bumped shoulders with his brother. "Whoa, you're blushing!"

Marco had turned eight shades of red. "I don't blush."

"Yeah, sure you don't," Tony chided.

Amy took a step back and smiled at Marco. "So, I've heard all about you."

Marco's chest visibly inflated. "I bet that was fascinating."

Amy nudged Tony. "He's as sarcastic as you are."

"This guy?" Marco asked. "I taught him everything he knows."

Just then Tony sneezed into his hand, then wiped the back of his hand on Marco's sleeve. It was a joke he loved doing in front of friends, but Emilia had hated it. Amy, he knew, would be different.

With a huge grin, she shook her head. "Your mother must be so proud of you."

Marco slung his arm over Amy's shoulder and whispered, "Can I clue you in? He's a deuce."

As his brother and his girlfriend goofed off, Tony's heart felt a lot lighter than it had in ages. He glanced at the family outside who were struggling with their belongings. "What's going on out there?" he asked.

Instantly Amy's voice lost all its playfulness. "You're not gonna believe this. They're moving in, and I have to share my room with my sisters."

Marco scoffed. "Oh, poor you. I have to share a room with deuce boy here."

Tony glared at him for being such a nitwit, but Amy laughed. With people losing their homes and jobs on Terminal Island, soon she would realize just how fortunate she was.

"If you're done being a comedian," Tony said to his brother, "we should go help those people."

* * * * *

Amy could not resist another game of patty-cake with Kim and her brother Ichi Aomori. They were such cute kids with their identical black bowl haircuts and sandals. So polite and well-behaved, except when they burst into uncontrollable fits of giggles, mostly at Amy's hands, as she tickled them just to hear their laughter. Whenever she did, Jasmine would pop her head in the room and put her fingers against her lips to quiet them. Amy would apologize, "My fault, my fault."

Mr. Hano Aomori was a hard-working, humble fisherman who had not yet mastered the basics of the English language, and his wife was no better. Still, their grateful smiles and bows said all they needed to about how much they appreciated the Kashiwagis' hospitality. After losing his home and boat, Hano had been left without shelter, a job, or a way to feed his family. Mr. Kashiwagi, having known Hano's family back in Japan, was eager to help.

The front door opened and Mr. Aomori walked in. Amy's father met him at the door, and Hano bowed, just as Amy had been taught to do when they had lived on Terminal Island fifteen years ago but never did anymore. Mr. Aomori said, "Konnichiwa sa, watashi—"

"Hano, please speak in English, even if it is not very good," Mr.

Kashiwagi instructed. "When I first came to America, I didn't know a word of English, and I went to a tutor. And I'll never forget something he said. 'Just as your command of the English language increases, your income will increase fourfold.' From that day forward, my wife and I adopted American mannerisms from the way I dress to the way I eat. We brought up our daughters as Americans. And my income did increase."

"Yes sir. I— I found a job," Mr. Aomori announced.

"Hano, I kn— knew— you would! Oh, Hano," Mrs. Aomori said, wiping tears from the corner of her eyes with a handkerchief.

Hano bowed once more to both Mr. and Mrs. Kashiwagi and stammered, "We'll m— move out n— next week."

Amy's father put a hand on his friend's shoulder. "No hurry," he said. "You're welcome here. What kind of job did you get?"

It was wonderful to see her parents laughing and smiling again. Then, a loud knock on the front door echoed through the living room. "Who could that be?" Amy's mother asked.

Mr. Kashiwagi opened the door, and two police officers stood there. Her father straightened his glasses. "May I help you?"

Without answering, one of the officers brushed Mr. Kashiwagi aside with his night stick, and the two entered. Amy had never seen her father manhandled before. "Dad!" she gasped, feeling sick to her stomach.

Mr. Kashiwagi held up his hand. "I really must insist that you— "

The taller of the two officers interrupted him. "We're here for illegal items."

"Illegal items?" her father replied, scanning around, arms out by his sides. "There's nothing like that here!"

The officers ignored him and searched the apartment, throwing open closets and drawers and exploring any possible hiding places. Pushing Mr. Aomori aside with brute force, they headed into the hallway, while the family stood there, powerless.

Amy tried making eye contact with her dad, hoping to gauge

the seriousness of whatever was going on, but he evaded her stare. Her mother, however, gave her a worried glance, as she rubbed her hands together.

Finally, the taller officer emerged from June's old bedroom, which was now occupied by Mr. and Mrs. Aomori. Triumphantly he held up an RCA radio transceiver, weathered and crusty from the salt air on Terminal Island. "Whose is this?" the officer demanded.

Mr. Aomori bowed slightly. "Is, is m— mine, po— policeman."

The officer handed the radio to his partner, then pulled out his handcuffs. His eyes narrowed with hatred. "You're under arrest." Turning to his partner, he spat out the next words with venom: "He's a spy." Then the police officer whirled Mr. Aomori around roughly and cuffed him without incident.

"You, you wr— wrong! I— I fish. Fisherman. In ocean, talk to— to my *wife*." Hano pleaded in his broken English, but the two cops paid him no mind. They pushed him out of the apartment to a backdrop of tears and sobbing.

Chapter 14

With each passing day, Tony's obsession with the war intensified. Every morning, he got up early, so he would have enough time to read the paper, and from his seat at the breakfast table, he kept his family alerted to the latest news. "Mom, listen to this," he said. Mrs. Piccinin could hardly hear over the sound of frying bacon. "The United States Government has frozen all bank accounts of any Japanese national or any citizen of Japanese ancestry."

"Sounds right to me," his mother said, turning the bacon.

Tony was taken aback. "What do you mean, sounds right? How are they gonna—"

"They should have thought of that before they bombed Pearl Harbor, Tony! They didn't give Primo a chance. Did they? Aren't you concerned about the Iarias?"

Just as Tony kept track of what was happening to the Japanese, Mrs. Piccinin was the unofficial historian for everyone in their Italian community who had enlisted, been wounded, killed, or otherwise affected by the war. Primo Iaria was four years older than Tony. His parents lived two doors down. Tony remembered him fondly, especially his easy-going nature. Primo had always let Tony and Paul play baseball with him and his friends. He was a sailor who had died at Pearl Harbor. His body was never recovered.

"Mom, I *am* concerned about the Iarias. But why are the Japanese being singled out? Why not us? The Italians? Or the Germans? You know, they're fighting against us, too,"

"We have our own worries. You might get called up! And, God forbid, I lost you." His mother flipped the bacon so hard that grease splattered everywhere. "And you want me to feel sorry for a few Japs who lost their money? My heart can only bear so much, Tony!"

* * * * *

Amy held the trashcan, dragging it around with her as she and her mother threw away anything that looked remotely Japanese. It was already half full after just a few minutes of purging, and now in the kitchen, Mrs. Kashiwagi dumped some chopsticks, which had not been used in years. Out went her father's sake cups and her mother's favorite teapot, then the bamboo place mats and the tiny frames featuring Asian symbols that hung over the dinner table, and all the Japanese prints that hung on the walls. Moving to the bedroom, out went the kimonos that her mother no longer wore, the sandals and the tabi, the traditional Japanese socks with the split between the toes.

Her mother wept throughout the whole process. Amy, never realizing just how much her family had held on to their old culture, marveled at how empty the apartment looked.

In the living room, she and her father hung an American flag from the window, so that it could be seen directly above the store sign. In two of the store windows, printed in big block letters so the police—and everyone else, for that matter—could see, they hung signs that read: *We Are Americans.* "That should be enough," Amy said, taping up the last sign.

"Hush," said Mr. Kashiwagi, staring out the store window. "For now, we do what we have to do. We can talk politics when the war is over." Then, in a gesture rare for her father, he touched her shoulder. "I'm sorry, Amy. These are hard times, and it might get worse. We must stick together, no arguments. Okay?"

She smiled and nodded. "Yes, Dad."

* * * * *

Through it all, Jasmine Aomori sat in her room with the shades pulled and her children shut out by the bolted door. When she finally came out, Ichi gazed up at her with his big brown eyes and asked, "When is Daddy coming back?"

"Soon," Jasmine lied, picking him up and settling him on her lap. "Soon. He— he see you soon." It was another nine months before Ichi would see his father again, and by then, he did not know who he was anymore.

* * * * *

In a sport coat and tie, Tony sat by the Christmas tree and counted the seconds till Amy arrived. His father and grandfather sipped wine, while Bing Crosby's Christmas album played on the phonograph. Marco shook his three presents, trying to figure out what he had coming the next morning. In the kitchen, Mrs. Piccinin, Angela, and Caterina cooked dinner, whispering about Amy, who was coming over for supper and Christmas Eve mass. Ever since his father insisted that Tony help Mr. Kashiwagi close the Terminal Island store, his mother's opinion of Amy did not matter anymore.

Through the window, Tony saw a car pull up. A moment later, Amy stepped out with a covered dish in her hands, and he ran out to greet her, taking the pan from her. Amy wore a cream-colored skirt and a green sweater over a white blouse, with her hair pulled back. Antonio and Grandpa Sansone stood when Amy entered the house, which Tony noted with pleasure. "Amy, this is my Grandpa that I have been telling you about."

"Merry Christmas," Grandpa said, bowing like they did in Italy when a woman entered the house. He winked at Tony and warbled a few lines from an Italian song, 'A Boy With A Beautiful Girl Always Sings'. Then he said to Amy, "I've heard so much about you. Let me get a good look at you! I must say, you're as pretty as my own granddaughters."

"Thank you," Amy said. "I never knew my own grandparents. Can I give you a hug?"

"Of course you can." He opened his arms to her. Tony could not have asked for a better welcome for his new girlfriend. *Thank God for Grandpa!*

But as Amy hugged him warmly, Tony overheard his mother in the kitchen. "Men are such fools. Look at that old coot, falling all over her."

"They have no sense," Caterina chimed in.

"You're a beautiful person," Grandpa said to Amy, wiping away his tears. "I'll always remember that." Then, his eyes fell on the container that Tony was holding. "What's in the pan?"

"Tiramisu," Amy answered. "A friend of mine from the store helped me."

"Tiramisu? I swear you're three-quarters Italian!" His grandfather turned to his son-in-law, beaming. "She made tiramisu!"

"Not on my table!" his mother hissed under her breath. Thankfully, Amy did not hear it, but Tony did. He shot his mother a vile look, which she ignored.

"I know. It's your favorite," his father replied, as he patted Grandpa on the back.

"Get these kids some wine," Grandpa announced to the whole room. "Christmas is a time for celebration."

While Mr. Piccinin poured two glasses of Dolcetto, Amy handed Marco a small wrapped package.

"Thanks! Can I open it now?"

"Yes. I hope you like it." she said, taking a glass of wine from Tony's father.

Marco tore the tissue paper off, and inside was a baseball card. "Dad, look! It's a 1909 Honus Wagner!" He paraded around the room, showing everyone to their delight. "You can't even find this in a collector's shop. Thanks, Amy. This is keen."

"Don't trade that one." Grandpa smiled. "It'll be worth a lot someday."

"I can't! It's a gift." Marco replied.

"Now remember that, when you're tempted," his father said.

In the kitchen, Angela scoffed for all to hear, "Look at 'em. All that over a stupid baseball card."

Marco looked at Amy. "How did you find this?"

Ignoring Angela's comment, Amy replied with a wink, "I have my ways."

Tony could not have been more proud of her. He wrapped an arm around her waist, pulled her in tight, and surprised her and everyone else with a quick kiss on the lips.

Chapter 15

A month had passed since the bombing of Pearl Harbor, and Tony kept up-to-date with the politics in both his state and in Washington D.C. Last week, CBS Radio had broadcast that Director J. Edgar Hoover at the Federal Bureau of Investigation and Attorney General Francis Biddle of the Justice Department had advised President Roosevelt against the need to detain the Japanese. Director Hoover was quoted, "They are not a security risk. We have already picked up those who are of high risk, and we will continue to do so."

But, in Sunday's newspaper, the *Los Angeles Times* reported that the California Growers Association had accused Japanese farmers of poisoning fruits and vegetables, putting America's food supply at risk. And just yesterday, Tony had read that California's Chamber of Commerce called for the removal of all Japanese, saying, "A Jap is a Jap."

Mr. Earl Warren, the Attorney General for the State of California, who was running for the Governor's office in the fall, was quoted as saying, "The Japanese situation as it exists in this state today may well be the Achilles heel of the entire civilian defense effort."

Farmers, businessmen, and local politicians acted as if it was their patriotic duty to run the Japanese out of California, but Tony suspected that their real desire was their farm land, their companies, and their constituents' vote.

Today, it really hit home when a story and photograph of Mr. Herbert Schultz at a Los Angeles City Council meeting made the front page of the *Times*. In the lead paragraph, he was quoted, "I call upon my fellow councilmen and citizens of this great city to unanimously support the political leaders of this terrific state in their call for the removal of all Japanese people to secure locations, where they will no longer be a threat to the safety of our country."

The influential newspaper commentator Walter Winchell added, "Herbert Schultz would be a great Mayor for the City of Los Angeles."

Tony slammed the paper down in disgust.

* * * * *

For Valentine's Day, Paul and his latest girlfriend, Nancy, doubled with Tony and Amy. The guys were dressed to the nines, and the girls had primped and preened all afternoon. Paul wore a charcoal gray sport coat accented with a silver tie and fedora, while his confrère donned a new double-breasted suit he bought with his pay from Coca-Cola. The girls looked nobby. Nancy was in a lemon chiffon evening dress with pearls, and Amy wore a teal lace cocktail dress.

Paul's mother had managed to book the last table at Capriccio's on Hollywood Boulevard for the foursome, thanks to her friend who knew the owner. The restaurant had opened four months ago and was the talk of the town. The food critic for the *Los Angeles Times* had already given it five stars for its exquisite signature dishes and impeccable service.

In the backseat of Tony's dad's car, Nancy was excited and could not stop talking. She scrunched next to Paul, touching and caressing him. It was going to be a great night.

Tony pulled up at the entrance, and Paul sprang to attention, helping his date out of the car. The parking lot was full, so Tony and Amy parked on the other side of the street.

Inside the restaurant, Paul and Nancy passed a few couples waiting for tables. With a smile, Paul approached the maître d'.

"Happy Valentine's Day! Two?" the maître d' asked.

"Four," he replied, feeling mature and sophisticated. "They're parking the car. We have reservations, in the name of Romano."

The steward looked at his list of reservations. "We'll get your table ready, sir. Please let me know when your guests arrive."

Stepping off to one side, Nancy gripped Paul's arm. "Why didn't you tell me?"

"Tell you what?"

"I couldn't very well say anything in the car," Nancy whined. "Tony's girlfriend—she's *Japanese*."

Before he could respond, Tony and Amy walked in, and Paul could not help but notice the odd looks the patrons were giving them. Feeling apprehensive, his muscles tightened as he approached the maître d'. "They're here," he said.

Looking up and seeing that Tony and Amy were in his party, the steward frowned and whispered to Paul, "May I speak to you privately, sir?"

"Um, sure," he replied.

* * * * *

Tony wondered why the maître d' was having a private conversation with Paul. Then, he noticed that everyone was staring at Amy. It could not possibly be *that* could it? Without warning, he heard Paul say a few choice words to the steward. With a tense look on his face, Paul walked back to his party.

Realizing what had happened, Tony said to the girls, "This place is all wet. Let's go somewhere else."

"Yeah, this place is for gunsels," Paul huffed. "Let's try someplace else."

"Why? I'm not going anywhere," Nancy decreed. "We have reservations, and I'm all dressed up. I'm not letting *her* ruin my night."

Amy winced in shock, and Tony saw it. "Come off it, Nancy. You know we'll take you someplace nice."

Paul joined in, "Yeah, someplace better than this overpriced joint."

But Nancy's face turned harsh and ugly. "Better than Capriccio's? Paul, it's the best place in town. And now this Jap has ruined it!"

Amy gasped, her hand to her chest, and Tony clenched his fists and lunged towards Nancy. He had no intention of hitting her, but the girl deserved a good scare—only Paul stepped over and blocked his path. "I'll take care of this." He took a ten-dollar bill from his pocket and flung it at her.

The money hit Nancy's dress and tumbled to the floor. "What the hell is this for?" she sneered, squatting and snatching it off the floor.

"A taxi," Paul said, getting some more money from his pocket. "Here." He threw the bills at Nancy's feet. "Get a life!" Red-faced, he pushed through the door and into the street.

"Shouldn't we—" Amy started to ask, but Tony grabbed her hand, and together they followed Paul. Her hand trembled as they walked out onto Hollywood Boulevard. It felt as if everyone was watching them. Two months ago, nobody would have cared if she was Japanese, but now everybody had an opinion, usually a negative one.

"I can't believe these people," Paul grumbled, crossing the street. "You'd think they'd never seen a Japanese person before."

Tony scurried after him, hustling Amy across the street, through thick traffic. An older couple in a beat-up coupe slowed down beside them. The wife drove with a cigarette dangling from her lips, and as Tony watched, her husband's face contorted into something strange and violent. Without warning, he stuck his torso out the window and threw a full beer bottle at them while screaming, "Traitor! Jap lover!" It crashed at their feet, spraying their legs with glass shards and beer.

"Tony!" Amy cried out.

"What the hell?" Tony yelled.

"Bastards!" shouted Paul, chasing after the car.

"Tony!" Amy called out again as he chased after them. In the heavy Saturday night traffic, the car did not get very far. Its brake lights blinked as it slowed. Or, at least, one of them did.

"Pull over!" Paul barked to the woman as he caught up with the car, ten yards ahead of Tony.

"Paul!" Tony called out, racing to catch up.

Suddenly, the car veered onto Highland Avenue and jerked to a stop in the middle of the street. The man, a big, beefy guy, lurched out with another bottle in his hand. His eyes were glassy and red, his gait unsteady, and his mouth hung open. "You want a piece of me?" he leered, waving a bottle at them.

His wife leaned out the driver's side window. "You tell him, Larry!" she slurred nastily.

From behind, Amy called out, "Don't! They don't know what they're doing!"

"Take it back!" Tony hissed. His fists were balled at his side.

"Like hell I will!" Larry shouted, taking a wild swing at him and sending himself off balance. Tony dodged the haymaker and tackled the man, breaking the bottle against the pavement. They wrestled on the ground, and Tony could tell he was stronger than his opponent who swung at him with the broken bottle, nicking a swath in his jacket.

Jumping up, Tony kicked the glass from the drunk's hand. "Apologize to her! Now!"

"Never!" the drunk vowed. "She's a little yellow whore!"

That was all it took for Tony to see a flash of red. Digging his shoes deep into the man's side, he kicked Larry, again, and again, as he punctuated every syllable, "Say— you're— sorry— you— drunk— bastard!"

"Tony!" Amy cried, trying to drag him away. "Stop! Tony! Stop!"

The wife shoved Amy away and yanked on Tony's hair. "Stop it!" she howled, scratching at his face and jumping onto his back. Tony pushed at her hands and shook her off like a dog with fleas.

Finally, Paul got ahold of Tony's arm and pulled him out of kicking range. "Jesus! What the hell got into you?"

Aware that a small crowd was forming, Tony staggered away. "C'mon," Paul said. "Let's get out of here." Amy closed in on his other side, and together they ushered him away—a good thing, or else he would have pummeled the man to death.

* * * * *

Trying to salvage the evening, Amy insisted that Paul go into Kashiwagi's Korner Market and get Debbie. After the store lights went out, they emerged together and strolled down the street, chatting animatedly. Tony and Amy were slumped down in the parked car, waiting for them, while Amy dabbed at the grazes on Tony's knuckles with a handkerchief.

Paul could not keep his eyes off Debbie in her knee-length skirt and snug sweater. While Amy was foreign and exotic, Debbie was tall, blond, and buxom. Tony and Amy watched them flirt as they approached the car. "Look at 'em. Ever since I met her, I knew she was right for him. I should've fixed them up weeks ago. They're like bread and butter," Amy said, squeezing Tony's hand.

"I thought we were bread and butter," Tony chided.

She turned to face him. He loved the way only half of her face was illuminated in the darkness of the car. "No, we're cake and icing. It's sweeter." She leaned up and kissed him on the cheek. "You okay?"

Tony sighed and closed his eyes. "Yeah, I'm sorry. It just burns me up."

"Are you still thinking about it?" Amy sighed. "You have to ignore it, Tony. Those people had nothing to do with you or me." She rested her head on his shoulder. "There's still three hours left of Valentine's Day. Let's have some fun tonight."

She reached up to him, offering a light kiss, and he leaned down to accept it. How much longer would life be this way? Tony felt an overwhelming need to take advantage of every second they spent together.

The back door of the car opened up, breaking them apart, and

Paul and Debbie slid into the backseat. Paul rested his arms on the backrest and looked at Amy. "You should've introduced me to this beautiful tomato a long time ago."

"I tried, but your social calendar is always so full," Amy back-chatted with a wink.

"That's because I'm in demand," Paul said, and the four of them laughed.

Putting the car in drive, Tony cruised away from the curb. "Where to?" he asked his passengers, as Paul and Debbie cozied up in the backseat.

Amy rested her left hand on Tony's thigh, a gesture that sent a surging fire shooting through his loins. "Turn right up here," she said quietly, to match the hushed tones oozing from the backseat. Tony lowered his hand onto his lap to camouflage his urgent outline, until the blaze burned out. "There's a little diner up the street with to-go boxes," Amy continued. "We could take a drive to Griffith Park and have Valentine's dinner up there."

They stopped at the eatery and ordered four Valentine specials to go. Tony did not care what was inside the little red boxes the owner handed over in a shopping bag, only that the night was saved and he was with people he cared about.

Tony drove to the hills on the north side of Los Angeles and entered Griffith Park. There were a few cars scattered about; he parked near the swing sets. "How romantic," he cracked.

"It is," Amy whispered, taking his hand and pressing her other hand over it. Tony thought about how different things would be right now had he still been dating Emilia. She never would have let him hear the end of it—ruining a perfect evening at Capriccio's—whereas Amy saw thing so differently. She did not carry on; she let things go. He was blessed, truly blessed, and he knew it.

"There's lots to do in the dark," Paul said from the back, his voice barely above a whisper. "Why don't we try some of them, Debbie?" Tony handed him two red boxes over the front seat, and Paul and a laughing Debbie slid from the car. Luckily, she was amenable to Paul's peculiar sense of humor.

Tony snuggled up close to Amy, sliding an arm around her waist, and she leaned her head on his shoulder. They watched as Paul and Debbie sank onto the swings next to each other. "Let's join them," she said. He was hoping to have her all to himself, but her exuberance was so infectious; how could he refuse? They got out of the car and went over to the playground.

"What gives?" Paul asked, as they joined them on the swings. "I thought it was time to get romantic."

"There's always time for romance," Amy said, kicking off in the sand and getting a head start. "But how often do you get to race to the top of the swing set?" Everyone joined in, swinging up and down, and back again with a breeze in their face, pushing higher and higher, till they could see the city lights below them.

As they were swinging, Tony wondered if there would always be time for love, happiness, and romance in this world. With all the uncertainty hanging in the air, he was not so sure anymore.

Chapter 16

Five days later, President Roosevelt signed Executive Order 9066 on February 19th of 1942. He declared one hundred-and-twenty thousand Japanese-Americans a threat to the security of the United States of America and ordered their immediate evacuation and deportation to ten relocation camps. The Kashiwagis had exactly three days to sell their grocery stores and settle their affairs.

As Amy lay in the middle of her bed, staring at the ceiling, refusing to move, she could not fathom how her family could be a threat to anybody. This was so unfair. She was born in this country. She was an American like everyone else.

* * * * *

In her bare room, once so gaily adorned with her postcard collection and photographs of family and friends, Amy packed silently with June and Kelly. There was little left for her to do but to slide the last of her possessions into her luggage. Underneath several blouses and skirts, Amy placed a black satin bag containing the stickpins Tony had given her.

It made her break into a fresh round of sobs. What would become of her and Tony? Where would she and her family live? She wanted to bang on the doors of the White House and beg President Roosevelt to please reconsider. But there was no use fighting. Maybe it would all be over soon, and before they knew it, their lives would return to normal.

Kelly struggled to fit all her toys and clothes into her single suitcase. She sat on it, bounced up and down on it, and broke into a fit of frustration. "Can you help me, Amy? Please?"

Wiping away her tears, Amy turned to June. "Can you help Kelly? I need to leave."

"I'll help you." June comforted Kelly, as Amy slid her arms into her plaid windbreaker. "Amy, do you think I'll ever be in love?"

"At a time like this, is that all you can think of?"

"Well, it just makes me wonder," June said. "Ever since you met Tony, you seem so different. You were happy before— I just mean different in a good way."

Amy saw the sad look in her sister's eyes and felt sorry for raining on her parade. "Just wait. Someday, you'll turn a corner, and he'll be standing right there."

"Just like that?" June asked.

"You'll see. It changes everything." Feeling better, Amy smiled at her sister.

* * * * *

Outside his store, Mr. Kashiwagi stood studying the contract in his hands as the cool February day seeped into his bones. Next to him, his wife stifled back tears. "What— what is this?" he asked Mr. Schultz who extended a black pen toward him. "You can't be serious?"

Mr. Schultz smirked. "I really wish you'd sold me your stores months ago when I first approached you."

"This isn't a sale," Mr. Kashiwagi sputtered. "It's a robbery." He wanted nothing more than to rip the contract and throw the pieces into this man's face, but he had no choice. Looking at the pen, he took it. Mrs. Kashiwagi was no longer able to contain her sobs. Hands trembling, he glanced down at the contract and hesitated, as the low, winter sun glinted off the pen cap.

"If you don't sell to me," Mr. Schultz reminded him, "the government will simply take possession. You'll get nothing. I'm doing you a favor paying you anything at all." His voice was as cold as the afternoon, but it was the truth. There were worse evils in the world than getting shortchanged. "Sign here," he instructed, pointing to the bottom of the contract.

"There's nothing we can do," Mrs. Kashiwagi said. Her voice was tired and weak, resigned to moving on, one way or another.

Without further hesitation, Mr. Kashiwagi placed the paper on top of the car and scratched out a violent signature. He set the pen on top of the paper and stormed back to the store. His eldest daughter was rushing out the door, the cowbell clanging above them. "Amy!" he barked as she stumbled into him. "Where do you think you're going?"

"Out!" she cried.

"No you're not. We need you here!" But Amy continued down the sidewalk. "I forbid you!" he shouted at her.

She turned around, crying. "You too? How much forbidding am I supposed to take? I can't take this anymore!"

He had never seen his daughter behave this way before. They faced extreme duress, but this was not the way to handle it. "When we need you the most, are you going to betray your family and leave?" he asked.

"What about what *I* need?" Amy turned on her heels and ran down the street.

Mrs. Kashiwagi appeared at his side, crying as well. "Let her go. She'll be back. She has nowhere else to go."

What is going on? All around him, Mr. Kashiwagi's world was collapsing—his country, his stores, and now his family. He reached for his wife's hand, just as a Coca-Cola delivery truck rumbled up to the curb. Mr. Piccinin stepped out, avoiding eye contact with the Kashiwagis. *What is he doing here?*

His old deliveryman headed straight to the back of his truck and began unloading. Walking over and pounding his shoulder, Mr. Schultz, in his overbearing salesman's voice, bellowed, "Antonio, thanks for coming. I want to make sure this store is well stocked." From his pocket, he pulled out a wad of cash. "Here." He pressed the money into his hand, "You know where to stack them."

Mr. Piccinin did not look comfortable with Mr. Schultz touching him, but he continued to unload as if his life depended on it. And maybe it did, Mr. Kashiwagi realized, as he looked on helplessly. For a second, the old friends locked eyes, and it seemed as though Mr. Piccinin begged his forgiveness. But just as quickly, it was gone.

* * * * *

Tony paced the little corner of the USC library where he and Amy usually met. His stomach was upset, as it always seemed to be these days. His dad did not want him seeing Amy anymore, for reasons obvious to him but incomprehensible to Tony, and Amy's father was being even more stubborn, yet they could not stay away from each other.

The world seemed horribly out of control. He was powerless to stop stupid people from making so many stupid decisions, powerless to control his family, and powerless to love whomever he felt like loving. Tony had never given much thought to what made him an American, or even what it meant to be an American. But the country he lived in now seemed far removed from the brave, idealistic nation he had learned about in his history books at school. To take property away from folks like the Kashiwagis, to turn friends into enemies, seemed ludicrous to him. How could anyone think a family like Amy's could betray the country? How could his mother and his sister Angela call Amy such foul, disgusting names?

He paced back and forth, avoiding eye contact with the reference librarian who seemed to know why he was there. Finally, Tony heard the squeaking of shoes behind him. He turned, spotting Amy. His heart plummeted seeing her in pain, her lovely face troubled by worry and doubt.

"Oh, Tony," she said, falling into his arms.

"Amy, I was so worried you wouldn't get away!" He held her, inhaling the lemony scent of her hair.

She hugged tighter. "Believe me. Nothing could stop me."

"Excuse me, young man," said the librarian from behind her desk. From the corner of his eye, he had seen her peering from underneath her glasses, giving them a disapproving look. Tony was tired of fighting his parents, her parents, and now the librarian, of all people. He took Amy's hand and led her out of the library.

They drove away from the City of Angels. If ever there were a need for angels, it was now. On the Pacific Coast Highway, they drove with the windows down, taking in the cold ocean winds and bright afternoon sun. At the crossroads of Malibu, they stopped at a secluded spot.

The glittering sea rolled and crashed under the sun, as it had for millions of years. Tony plucked a blanket from the car's trunk and guided Amy to a clearing. Together they laid it out flat, then sank into its softness.

Amy sighed, nestling her head against Tony's shoulder. "I wish we could stay here forever. It's so beautiful."

"Like you," he said, gazing down at her.

"You're too nice to me," she said, slapping his leg playfully. "Why can't anyone understand what you mean to me? Why is the world trying to ruin our happiness? I don't understand it."

"Just let 'em try," Tony berated, nostrils flaring. Nothing had been able to stop them so far. Nobody ever would, he was sure of it.

She sighed and patted his knee. "Not now. Let's just make this moment last." And so they snuggled in each other's arms, letting the sea and the wind wash away their weariness.

After a while, Tony remembered something. He reached into the pocket of his letterman's jacket. "I have a gift for you."

Amy sat up and watched as he unwrapped the crinkly tissue in his hands to reveal a Japanese stickpin he had found that weekend at a secondhand store. "Is this it?" he asked, searching her dark brown eyes. He knew even before she shook her head no, that it was not.

He held his palm open, admiring the slow, sensual way she drew it out of his hand, then placed it in her hair. "I want you to know

I'll never quit looking."

"I know." She slid into his arms, angling her head slightly so that their lips met, so sensual and warm.

When at last they pulled away in the waning afternoon light, he asked, "Can I tell you something?" He rested his cheek in her hair. "On Hallowe'en, do you remember the dog?"

Amy nodded slowly. "Yeah."

"Well, that night, I couldn't sleep. All I could think about was our date. I remember everything, every detail. But for some reason, I always came back to that dog. Remember, how the guy had to drag the dog out?"

"Yeah."

"Well, that dog knew he was better off with you. I'll never forget that. Two minutes, and he knew. At three in the morning, it came to me. I'm better off with you."

Amy looked up at him. "Are you saying you're a dog, Tony Piccinin?" she joked.

"Very funny, little girl," he said, tickling her side.

Amy laughed, then kissed him. "My turn," she said. "Remember when you whistled for my attention in the store, and all the walls shook?"

He shoved her away playfully. "Come on, it wasn't that bad."

She laughed. "Yes, it was. Bottles broke."

"Now you're exaggerating."

Her intoxicating laughter echoed off the cliff walls. "No I'm not. It was worse than an earthquake."

Teasing her, Tony pursed his lips to whistle. "Don't," she gushed, covering his lips with her hand. "They'll hear you on Catalina."

Tony wrapped his arms around her and held her close again. "What am I gonna do with you?" His voice cracked with the thought of losing her. She pulled into him tighter. He felt her body tremble and then, silently, she began to sob.

He held her tight and let it all out as well, not caring how hard his tears came.

* * * * *

When Tony opened the kitchen door, his parents sat at the table drinking tea. From the look on his mother's face, he knew she was about to start in on him. And he was right. "You were out with that Jap girl, weren't you?" Surprisingly, his father glared at his mother, but when Tony did not answer, she huffed, "You didn't do anything rash. Did you?"

"Maria, now isn't the time," Antonio said.

"No, Mom. And I bet you're happy," Tony answered, slamming his fist against the wall, as he walked away.

"Happy has nothing to do with it. Don't you dare leave when I'm talking to you!"

Turning off the hall light, he closed his bedroom door.

* * * * *

Outside, the rain came down in sheets, as Maria stood over the stove and made breakfast as usual. Tony sat with his head on the table, and Caterina read a *Dick and Jane* book next to him. The door opened, letting in an icy gust, and Marco hurried in. Droplets from his raincoat fell onto the floor as he placed today's paper next to Tony's head.

"Did everyone get a paper?" their mother asked.

"Yes, Mom, everyone got a paper," Marco droned, hanging his raincoat on the peg and sitting down with his siblings at the table.

"Is your algebra done?" Caterina asked, needling him.

Marco grabbed her and rubbed his knuckles on her head. "Why you little squirt! What do you care about my algebra? Huh, huh?"

"Mom, make him stop!" Caterina laughed.

Angela shuffled in, schoolbooks clutched to her chest. Her gaze fell on Tony, who was slumped over in his chair. "What's wrong with him?"

"That hurts," Caterina said, squirming in her chair.

Mrs. Piccinin gave a curt response. "Angela, mind your own business."

"It's not supposed to tickle," Marco chuckled.

Tony scanned the room. He watched Marco and Caterina having a tickling fight and felt like he was in the wrong house, like he had been born into the wrong family. Did they not realize what was happening outside their door? Did they not care about the injustices going on right in their own city?

Angela placed her books on the counter and locked eyes with Tony. "Where's Amy going?" And there it was. She was the only person brave enough to ask what they all were thinking.

Maria dropped her spatula on the counter and Marco and Caterina stopped playing to look at Tony, awaiting his response. But before he could answer, his mother slapped Angela on the mouth. "Go to your room!" she commanded.

"I was just being nice!" Angela wailed at her mother, bursting into tears, fleeing the kitchen.

"And don't come back 'til you're ready to apologize to Tony!" his mother yapped.

Chapter 17

Amy stood in line, suitcase at her feet, as rain seeped down her back. The Kashiwagis had tugged their rain gear from the bottom of their luggage an hour earlier, when the clouds threatened and the thunder came, but by now, the heavy downpour had soaked through everything they wore, leaving them damp and impatient. The line in downtown Los Angeles stretched for blocks.

Her father led their group and next to him stood her mother. A simple black umbrella deflected some droplets from her shoulders and head. Then Mrs. Aomori and her children took their place. Behind them were Amy and her sisters.

The rain was endless, and the humbly-dressed families around them clung to their few possessions, mumbling quietly about the future, the past, but not the present—God, anything but the present.

The Kashiwagis and Aomoris crept forward, a few feet every few minutes, as families at the front of the line trudged off to the buses. Amy studied the soldiers in their weather gear, rifles over their shoulders, checking the families in. She had never been this close to a gun before, let alone a dozen or more. The soldiers and their hostile stares frightened her. She kept her sisters close, picturing one of them inching out of line for something innocent, like tying her shoelaces, only to have a soldier fill her full of lead. Maybe that was just her imagination, but the threat of violence lingered in the air.

Three hours later, they were at the front of the line. Dripping wet, Mr. Kashiwagi stepped forward. A fresh-faced soldier, not much older than the USC students who used to come into his store, looked down at his clipboard, pen hovering over it. "Last name?" he barked.

Her father's voice was low and proud as he answered, "Kashiwagi." The soldier's eyes did not move from his clipboard. He traced his pen down the list, spelling the name out as he went, or at least, the part he understood: "K-A-S-H." At last he looked up. There was an indifference to his flat gaze. He used the pen to point to their left. "The buses for Manzanar are over there."

For a moment, Amy imagined her father letting them have it, raging about the injustice befalling him and his family, declaring this whole act immoral and inhuman, but Mr. Kashiwagi meekly slid to one side. "Ah, yes. Thank you," he said.

Mrs. Aomori stepped forward.

"Last name?" the soldier snarled.

"Aomori." Mrs. Aomori bowed.

The soldier looked up, water dancing on his rain gear. "Spell it."

"A-O-M-O-R-I."

The soldier went down the list, mouthing the letters "A-O-M. The group for Jerome is over there. Your buses will be here this afternoon."

Mr. Kashiwagi leaned over slightly, addressing the soldier with respect. "Ah, yes, excuse me, sir. Where's Jerome?"

"Ar-kansas," the soldier said, as the whole family drew near to hear him. "Wherever that is."

"Arkansas?" her father corrected his pronunciation, shaking his head. "Sir, no, please. That's a mistake. She's by herself. Can she go—"

"Army regulations." The soldier merely shook his head, water cascading off the brim of his cap. "Next!" he called over Mr. Kashiwagi's shoulder.

Before Mr. Kashiwagi could argue his case, the soldier growled at the next family in line, "Last name?" It was done. He was done. Mr. Kashiwagi turned to Mrs. Aomori with a dismal look.

Mrs. Aomori broke down in tears. Amy took her hands. "We'll

write you, wherever you are," she said, just as she had promised Tony the night before.

Mrs. Aomori nodded, then led her children away to the staging area that would eventually take them to Arkansas. "So far away," said Amy's mother, seizing her husband's arm. "Will we ever see them again?"

He had no answer.

*****

From the bus window, a mass of makeshift buildings and tents rumbled into view on the desert floor. Amy braced herself as she spied the ominous barbed wire fences and guard towers. Approaching the prison, the air became clogged with miniature clouds of dust. The land had been scraped clean of sagebrush and vegetation. Not one blade of grass or a single plant was left to hold the dirt in place.

The bus's battered shocks caused the massive vehicle to lurch forward before it rocked into place, shuddering to a stop. Amy groaned and rubbed her neck. Except for one stop, when everyone had disembarked to relieve themselves in the open air, she had sat next to her sisters on a bench seat for eight hours on the jam-packed bus. Her back was sore and her legs were cramping. Everyone crowded the thin aisle between the seats, hoisting luggage, bags, and wraps as they shuffled, anxiously, off the bus.

A long, low building, smelling as if it had just been built in the last week or so, with soldiers on both sides of the door, beckoned them in. Amy held Kelly's hand as the Kashiwagis shuffled into the chicken coop of a building and joined another line of grumpy, tired families. The low ceiling gave the impression that the flimsy structure was smaller than it was. The few windows made it dark save for the bare light bulbs stretched along the ceiling. Somewhere a loudspeaker squawked to life, and Amy winced as a voice broke in: "Please have your bags ready for inspection."

"What does 'inspection' mean?" Kelly asked.

"It means they want to go through your stuff," June huffed, just before Mrs. Kashiwagi shushed them.

There were long tables with several officers in stiff green uniforms behind them. "Line up, line up!" voices shouted, indistinguishable from one another. "Find an open space and place your belongings on top."

Mr. Kashiwagi led his family to an open table where three soldiers spoke to each other. Amy read the names sewn into their shirts. Corporals Lett, Duffy, and Nagy were young, rough, and brutish in their appearance. They had an obnoxious air about them, not unlike some of the football players and fraternity boys who had come into Kashiwagi's Korner Market from time to time, staying too long and behaving as if they owned the place.

Immediately, their stares fell upon Amy. Blushing, and aware of how the rain and now sweat had made her clothes cling to her slender body, she pulled her sisters close, as their father slid their luggage piece by piece onto the table.

Corporal Nagy opened Amy's suitcase and searched the contents with his thick, Midwestern fingers. He paused on something white and shiny, and Amy held her breath, hoping he would move along. But instead, he held up her nightgown, showing it to Corporal Lett. "Look what we have here!" he said, ogling the garment. Amy glanced at her father for support, but he was busy arguing with Corporal Duffy who had confiscated his camera. "Remind me to find out what cabin you're in, doll, and I'll tuck you in real good." He laughed, and Amy fought the urge to turn around and run.

"Hey!" June snapped, for once bolder than her sister. "That's none of your business. You better put that back before I—"

"Oh, we have a live one here." Corporal Lett chuckled.

Amy tugged June close and whispered in her ear. "They're just joking," she lied through gritted teeth, hating that June knew she was lying, and nodded anyway.

Others were looking now, families to the left, to the right, both sides—the Japanese and the Army men—watching how she would react. Amy felt the blush rise to her cheeks as Corporal Nagy rifled through her dresses and skirts, yanking out a pair of pink cotton panties. Holding them up, he admired them in front of his friends, Corporals Lett and Duffy, standing nearby.

"Excuse me," Amy blurted, "but those aren't your size."

The Japanese families around her laughed, nudging her on the shoulder, while Corporals Lett and Duffy guffawed and slapped Nagy on the shoulders. "Yeah, those aren't your size, Corporal!"

Corporal Nagy shoved the underwear back in her luggage and glared at her. "What's your name?"

She did not like the way he asked, but now she was stuck having to answer his question. June clutched her hand. "Amy Kashiwagi."

His brown eyes pinned her with a cold stare. "I'll remember you," he warned, digging even deeper into Amy's suitcase.

She turned to find her father scowling at her, as though she were the troublemaker here, not the perfect stranger who just had her most private belongings displayed for the world to see. Would it be so hard for him to defend her for once?

"What do we have here?" Amy turned to find Corporal Nagy fondling the black satin bag containing her stickpin collection.

No, please not those, Amy wanted to say, but she kept her mouth shut this time.

"What're these?" he asked, untying the red cinch tie and sliding out one of the elegant pins with the jade top. He poked his finger on the sharp end. "Ow!" he mocked. "No weapons allowed."

"It's a stickpin, not a weapon," Amy protested.

Corporal Nagy gave her a look, warning her to be quiet. Then, he slid her luggage forward, placing the satin bag into a box next to him. Inside were radios, cameras, jewelry and, now, her stickpins.

"Sir, those are mine. They're harmless. They're for my hair. Please—"

"You'll do well to keep your mouth shut, Miss Kashywaguy."

What was wrong with these people? Why was she being treated

so unfairly? Clearly, a young woman and her stickpins had nothing to do with the incident at Pearl Harbor. As Corporal Nagy turned to Corporal Duffy to laugh about something, Amy pulled out the stickpin that was in her hair and hid it in her dress pocket before Nagy could notice.

"Come on," she said to her sisters, dragging them along as her father led the way. As they carried their suitcases, the Kashiwagis hid their faces in the crooks of their arms to provide protection against the sand, dust, and bits of rock the winds hurled against them. The gusts were filled with malice, directing their rage against the family, and the sand and dirt felt like tiny bullets striking their legs and backs. Even the sky was gray and angry, like a predator that had lost the scent of its prey.

Making their way through an encampment devoid of any color, Kelly gripped Amy's hand harder. "Is it always like this?" she asked.

"Kelly? Guess what?" Mrs. Kashiwagi said in a tone to distract her. Amy recognized the technique. Her mother had used the same voice on her years ago. "Spring is coming. It's your favorite time of the year."

"But where's our home?" Kelly asked, unwilling to be diverted.

"We're coming to it. We'll make our place special. Don't you worry," her mother said with a forced smile.

In the middle of the street, the Kashiwagis passed several people filling their mattresses with hay. "What are they doing?" Kelly asked.

"Sweetheart, we're almost there," Mrs. Kashiwagi replied.

* * * * *

As they stepped into their 500-square foot cell, a massive cloud of despair followed the Kashiwagi family inside. Looking at the meager surroundings, Amy clutched her stomach, feeling as though its contents would escape at any second. The walls and ceiling had no drywall, just studs and joints. An oil heater in the corner, a dangling bulb, bed frames and empty mattresses furnished the room.

"Is this it? Look! You can see the ground between the floor boards!" Amy exclaimed. She imagined Tony with her, seeing what she was seeing, appalled at the living quarters, taking her and driving far, far away from here.

"Where's the bathroom and kitchen?" Kelly asked.

Rustlings and other movements came from behind the thin walls. June glanced toward them. "Listen, you can hear next door," she said, her eyes brimming with tears.

Amy placed an arm around her shoulder. "It's okay, June. It's only temporary." But Amy's intuition told her it would be a long time before they got out of here. While she did not blame her mom and dad, she did hate her parents' homeland for causing this horror.

Amy shivered, looking around the desolate room again. Not only did the lack of furnishings bother her—she knew that a home was more than table and chairs—it was also memories and family. Intangible elements made a house a home, but here the ambience was as barren as the walls.

"Amy, please take your sisters and find me a broom," her mother ordered, valiantly holding back what Amy was sure were tears. "A lady said there's a supply store."

Outside, while looking for the commissary, the girls investigated the grounds of the concentration camp. Kelly looked around at her bleak surroundings with utter dismay. "I don't like it here."

"Everyone shares your feelings, Kelly," June replied. "No one would like it here."

"You can make new friends," Amy said, anxious to reassure the nine-year-old. "I'm sure there are kids your age to play with."

"But I like my *old* friends," Kelly said. Tears overflowed from her lower eyelids. Amy reached out and blotted them with her handkerchief.

Spotting a mess hall, the girls ventured inside. What they found was even worse than their living quarters. There were bare, unvarnished tables and rows and rows of hard, wooden planks for seating. Piles of garbage lined the back wall.

"We have to eat here? No wonder they call this a 'mess' hall," June commented, causing Amy to crack the tiniest of smiles.

"Gross! I won't eat there," Kelly said, making a face.

"You will when you get hungry enough," June said, as Amy led her sisters back outside.

They walked around quietly. There was nothing to say. Tears rose in June's eyes and flowed down her cheeks. "This is awful. It's a nightmare. Only we're awake and living it."

Amy grabbed June's hand. "Don't think like that. As soon as the war is over, we'll get our lives back. You have to hang onto that."

"What if the war lasts forever?" June broke into a fresh wave of sobs.

"No! We'll have none of that," Amy said, sounding exactly like her mother. As much as her mom's scolding had annoyed her in the past, she was surprised to sound like her now.

They continued on in silence, not sure where they were headed; only praying it would get better. Their quiet was broken only by their own gasps when they entered the women's restroom. Dust and grime spotted the floor. The toilets and showers had no partitions. Water ran along the floor, pooling in mud holes, and the smell was anything but sterile. Several women were showering in small groups, trying to make the best of the meager trickles of water that came out of the shower heads.

Out of respect for their privacy, Amy averted her eyes and found her little sister gawking. "Kelly, don't stare," she admonished. Kelly turned her face into her oldest sister's side.

June gaped, "I'm never going to use the bathroom again."

Kelly started crying. "I've got to pee." Her sisters took her to the toilet, but she would not stop crying and urinate until they formed a fortress of modesty around her.

* * * * *

Corporals Nagy, Duffy, and Lett crowed over their loot the way pirates gloated over their treasure. Japanese swords, rare metals, cameras, radios, and anything else of value were all packed into boxes.

"Not bad, not bad at all," Nagy said, wiping his hands with glee.

"Talk about easy pickin's. It was easier than shootin' fish in a barrel," Duffy sniggered.

"Did you see me take these candlesticks from that old Jap?" Lett asked, eager to prove he was the best thief. "Damn! The government should have let the Japs bring more stuff with them."

Lett taped down a corner of a box. "Anything else to pack up?"

"Nope, we got it all," Nagy answered, lifting a heavy box in his arms.

They hauled the boxes out and hoisted them onto an Army truck already stocked with cigarettes, sugar and coffee. In a Private's uniform, Jeff Schultz headed over to them from the main building and smiled like a gangster—wide and full of evil. He had enlisted at the end of the fall semester and, with his father's connections, had been assigned a noncombat position, running errands for the draft board. "Nice going," he said, handing Corporal Lett a stack of bills. The corporal counted the cash.

"What, don't you trust me?"

Lett tallied the money. "You? Not a bit!"

"When's the next group?" Jeff asked, climbing into the truck.

"Friday."

"I'll see you then."

Annoyed, Lett looked up. "Hey, you're two hundred short! Where's the rest?"

"I'll have it on Friday. I promise." Schultz started the engine and drove off, leaving a trail of dust behind him.

"That chiseler! He's just like his old man," Lett said, slapping the bills with his hand. "God, I'm ready for Reno!"

"I can already smell the broads!" Duffy guffawed.

Lett punched his arm. "Don't be crass. They're expensive

whores," he said, cackling at his own joke.

Chapter 18

Blankets, strung on wires, divided the Kashiwagis' cell into three cramped rooms—a living room, the girls' bedroom, and their bedroom. Used, battered furniture gave the place a semblance of a house.

With a towel over his shoulder, shampoo and soap in hand, Mr. Kashiwagi departed for the men's restroom, as Mrs. Kashiwagi swept the endless streams of dust that seeped in through the floor boards.

In the girls' bedroom, Amy had decorated the studs with her postcard collection. It did not look quite the same as at home, but it would have to suffice for now. Sitting on her bed, Amy took out a sheet of stationery. There was still an outside world. Someday, they would return home, and life would begin again. That was what she had told her sisters, and that was what she must believe.

"Dear Tony," she began. She wrote and wrote, pouring her heart out about how much she missed him and telling him everything that had happened since their tearful farewell.

After finishing the letter, Amy took it in an unsealed envelope to the post office where Corporal Nagy was taking a black marker to letter after letter. "I'd like to mail this, please."

Nagy studied her for a few seconds, then flashed a sinister smile. "I remember you, you're Amy Kashywaguy. Has anyone ever told you that you're kinda pretty for a Jap girl?"

Amy's veins turned to ice. How could he talk to her that way when he knew what she and her family were going through? Did he not care that they had lost everything?

"Turn around. C'mon, turn around. I want to see what the other side looks like," he said, leering at her.

Amy set her letter and envelope on the counter and left without another word.

* * * * *

As Tony and Paul walked into the bedroom, Tony put his schoolbooks on his dresser, then threw himself on his bed. "How was your date with Debbie last night?" he asked, not that he gave a damn. God, it had been ten days since he had last seen Amy, and already his heart ached.

With a devilish smile, Paul said, "Well, let's just say I don't know what movie we saw, if you get my drift." He grabbed a baseball off the nightstand and tossed it back and forth from one hand to the other.

"You and your one-track mind," Tony mumbled.

"Yeah, like you wouldn't do—"

Tony spotted two letters on his desk and did not hear what else Paul had to say. The top one was in Amy's writing. He jumped up and tore it open. "Look at this!" he cried, shoving the letter in front of Paul's eyes so he could see the black censor bars running through it. "That wasn't necessary! She isn't revealing any national secrets. Hell, she doesn't even *know* any national secrets!"

Tony devoured Amy's few uncensored words. "She needs feminine products and winter coats. Damn, some jerk took her stickpins. What an ass! He claimed they could be used as weapons. Can you believe that?"

Paul scanned the other envelope. "When you finish that, you'd better read this." He held it up. The return address was the United States Army.

Tony snatched it from his hands, opened it and read it, open-mouthed. It was his draft notification. "It's official, I'm in the Army."

"I bet mine's at home," Paul said. "Are you ready for this?"

"Not really. Are you?"

"God has to protect me," Paul said. "You know, my uncle."

"Father Romano can't save you. You have to be tough, like me," Tony said, grabbing Paul and putting him in a headlock as Marco walked in.

"Girls, girls, no grab-assing," Marco said. Tony and Paul turned on Marco, tackling him. The three of them tumbled to the floor and howled. It was the first time Tony had laughed since Amy was taken away, and it felt really good.

* * * * *

The second-hand store offered quality goods at cut-rate prices that Tony could afford. A clerk, wearing a tag on his shirt that said "Chinese", approached Tony, Paul, and Marco as they entered the store. "I help," the clerk said.

"Women's coats?" Tony asked, looking around.

"Back wall."

"Why the tag?" he asked the clerk, pointing to his shirt.

Drawing his eyebrows together, the clerk looked down at the tag. "I not belong in concentration camp. I Chinese."

Tony gulped. He hadn't heard the term "concentration camp" in this context before—Manzanar had been referred to as a "War Relocation Center" in the newspapers. So Amy had been sent to a *concentration camp*? Tony felt sick to his stomach, imagining her in a bleak encampment, withering away.

They headed to the back wall, and Tony selected four women's winter coats in different sizes. The last was plaid, matching Amy's windbreaker.

Their next stop was the grocery store to purchase feminine pads. The boys found the appropriate section, but they waited while a girl from their school eyed them suspiciously before she selected her products and left.

"How many are you buying?" Paul asked, holding up some of

the various choices and tossing them to Marco, who tried to avoid them.

"I don't know," Tony answered. "How many do you think they use?"

Paul slapped Marco on the shoulder. "How many did you use last month?"

"Does that include the ones you borrowed?" Marco retorted, walking away.

"Don't leave! Pay for them, and your brother will give you a dollar."

"No way! Five!" Marco demanded.

"You're on," Tony said.

"You're so gross," Marco said, leaving the store.

* * * * *

Back home, Tony undid the stitching in the armpit of the plaid coat. He inserted a stickpin inside and sewed it back up. He packed all the coats in a cardboard box and taped a letter he had written to the package. Tony had ended the letter with: *"Amy, always remember that I love you and when this is over I am coming for you. I will see you soon. With my deepest love, Tony. P.S. If you ever feel a poke, that's me."*

* * * * *

When Corporal Nagy handed Amy the large box, she smiled for the first time in weeks. She tried to smile to be strong for her sisters, to speak in a firm, uplifting tone to give them hope, but she knew they could see right through her. But when she saw the box, she smiled naturally. Carrying it home, she literally hugged the package, as if it were Tony.

When she walked into her family's cell, the others were freezing in their light jackets around the small oil heater. With a big grin, Amy plopped the box down. "Mr. and Mrs. Piccinin sent us coats."

"Really?" June exclaimed, jumping up to help her.

Together, they ripped open the box and were awed when they pulled out winter coats. These were garments they had never needed when they lived in Southern California. Kelly and June each put on a jacket, as did their mom. Amy pulled out Tony's high school letterman's jacket and held it to her face, inhaling what remained of his familiar Old Spice scent.

Even though her parents were watching, she could do nothing to hide her tears. It smelled like him, it felt like him in her arms, and for all intents and purposes, it *was* him at that moment. When she looked up, her whole family was staring at her. Even her father had a shadow of remorse in his eyes. Amy noticed the note taped to the front of the jacket: *For Mr. Kashiwagi.* "Dad, it's for you," she said, handing him the jacket.

Her father stared at the handwriting, as though he were remembering every time he had been unkind and unfair to the boy whose jacket he now held. He swallowed, initially fighting the need to put it on, then relented, slipping it on. "He's a good boy," he said as he opened the door and left.

"Mom, how do I look?" Kelly asked, twirling around in her coat.

"Good. June, that looks terrific on you. Mrs. Piccinin did a wonderful job," her mother said.

"Look, it matches her jacket!" Kelly pointed to the coat that Amy took from the bottom of the box and put on.

Mrs. Kashiwagi inspected Amy's jacket. "I see Mrs. Piccinin had some help. Let's trade. This coat might fit you better."

Amy was not sure. She preferred the plaid coat, but she respectfully did as her mother asked, trading the plaid for the darker, plain coat.

"Let's see. You look—," her mother began.

"Mom, they're the same size. Can I please have that one back?" she asked, slipping her arms out of the plain coat.

"It's just a coat," her mother insisted, while a few fiery stares flew back and forth.

"I know. Can I please—"

"Amy, it's time to move on! You know, it's over between you and him," her mother said, clearly annoyed. It was not that her mother wanted to hurt her—she could tell from her expression that this was about accepting the truth. Things had changed and she would never see Tony again.

"That's what you think!" Out of frustration, Amy scurried to the door.

Behind her, her mother echoed, "Fine. Learn the hard way!"

As Amy opened the door to leave, she was met by a couple in their sixties, wearing cashmere overcoats. Mr. Kashiwagi, back from his walk, came up to them. "May I help you?"

The couple bowed. Her father bowed back. "We've been assigned to this apartment," the man said, handing him several official looking papers. "My name is Senri Fukuoka, and this is my wife, Keiko."

Mr. Kashiwagi said nothing. Amy could see exactly the same thoughts as hers running through his mind: *Where would they sleep? What would happen to their privacy?*

But as usual, her father's decency took precedence. "Come in," he said, helping them with their leather suitcases. "We have plenty of room."

As they stepped into the already cramped room, Kelly looked at her mother. "Where will they sleep?"

"We'll make room," Mr. Kashiwagi said, eyeing his youngest child.

* * * * *

Bundled in the ugly, plain coat, Amy lay on top of the triple-bunk bed, finishing Tony's letter. Below her, in the plaid jacket, Mrs. Kashiwagi swept the floor. Amy concluded the letter with: *"P.S. Can you believe it? Mom is already getting the coat dirty!"*

As she prepared to mail the letter, Mrs. Fukuoka opened the

door. "Child, take my scarf. You need to cover up. It's cold outside." As she handed her the wrap, Mrs. Fukuoka noticed the ornament in Amy's hair. "That's a pretty stickpin."

"Thank you. That's nice of you to notice." Amy draped the scarf around her neck. "I'll be back in a bit."

Once again, Corporal Nagy was the only person in the post office. Amy almost turned around and left right then, but her desire to mail the letter overcame her revulsion for the lecherous soldier. She decided she did not care what he had to say to her. She would just ignore it.

As she approached the counter, he grinned and asked, "Are you still writing to a white boy? You know he's using you, don't you?"

Amy paid him no mind. He was only saying these things to pester her, and the more she ignored him, the stronger she became. She handed him the unsealed letter. He held up his black marker and bared his teeth like a jackal before dismantling its helpless prey. "With or without the marks?" Nagy teased.

Amy ignored him.

"Hey, I'm trying to help you!" he said.

It had not occurred to her until that moment, that, even though Corporal Nagy was in the better position, they were both forced to be there. He had to spend every day in this desert hellhole, just like she did. She almost felt sorry for him.

"Look," he said, reaching under the counter. He brought up a bottle of sake and a gold wristwatch. "See what others have given me. Come here. I know what you can give me, and it doesn't cost a dime."

What is he saying? I would never give him anything.

"I said come here!" he commanded.

Amy felt the urgency in his voice. She turned and walked away.

Infuriated, Nagy raised his voice. "Dammit! Come here!" All at once, he rushed her, spinning her around. "You damn Jap! You think you're too good for me, don't you? You don't know what I can do for you!"

Amy struggled against his hands, which gripped her wrists,

hurting her. Nagy pinned her against the wall and pressed his mouth against hers.

"Stop it," she cried, pushing against him, but he held her firmly against the wall.

"Stop what? I'm your boyfriend now," he said, unbuttoning her coat, then her blouse.

"STOP!" she yelled again, as he pushed up her brassiere and squeezed her breasts. Struggling against his strength, she tried to knee him in the groin, push him off, scratch his face—anything—but she was no match for his formidable strength. With all of his might, he squashed his whole body against hers, and she felt his erection pressing underneath his trousers. When Nagy lowered both of his hands and lifted her skirt, Amy raised her hand to get the stickpin. But it was out-of-reach. As he yanked her panties down, she frantically tried her other hand. It worked. She pulled the stickpin out of her hair. While Nagy touched her private parts, Amy reached up and slammed it down with as much force as she could muster, imbedding the stickpin deep into his cheek.

Nagy screamed in pain; blood ran down his face in rivulets. Amy slipped out of his grasp and tripped. She yanked her underwear up and ran out of the building, gasping for air. Outside, several people stared at her until she realized she was still exposed. She pulled her coat over her and straightened her undergarments.

As Amy raced back to the hovel, a squadron of Air Force planes dove low over the camp. People were running, hitting the ground, and covering up their heads. As Amy neared her cell, Mrs. Fukuoka rushed outside, eyes to the sky. "What's going on?"

"It's nothing," Amy panted, leading her back inside. "Those halfwits have done that three times since we arrived." She closed the door and lowered the makeshift curtains over their only window.

"There is no call for scaring people," Mrs. Fukuoka said in disgust.

Amy removed the scarf, and her hands trembled as she returned it.

"What is it, child? You're shaking."

"Nothing. Everything. I hate it here!" Amy shook as the tears flowed down her cheeks. Mrs. Fukuoka took her in her arms and held her tight.

"It's okay, dear. Everything will be all right."

Walking into the room to see what all the commotion was about, Mrs. Kashiwagi saw Mrs. Fukuoka consoling her overwrought daughter. She retreated back to her partition.

Chapter 19

Tony ran inside the house. "Hello? Anybody home?" he shouted, ignoring his graduation cake sitting on the kitchen table. It seemed so insignificant now. He rifled through the mail on the kitchen counter, but there was still no word from Amy. Strange, she had promised she would write. He tossed the stack of letters onto the table, and they slid into the cake, getting butter cream on the corner of the envelopes.

Miffed as to where everybody was, Tony walked into his room. "Surprise!" his family yelled, clapping and giving him hugs he wished he could feel.

"You're the first Piccinin to ever finish high school!" Angela announced. Tony smiled and pretended to care, but all he really wanted was a letter, just one more letter from Amy before he left.

* * * * *

Walking through the train station, Tony and Paul absorbed the sobs and the pats on the back. The Piccinins, the Romanos, and Paul's girl, Debbie, were all there to see them off, with plenty of tears, hugs, and kisses. The place was abuzz with noise as grandsons, sons, brothers, and boyfriends headed out to fight the war. Tony and Paul were taking the train to Fort Benning for basic training.

Everyone was overcome with emotion, but Tony. He found it annoying. He still had his freedom, but what about Amy and her family? No one was crying over them.

As he and Paul made their way to the train, a few girls tossed flowers at them. Other soon-to-be soldiers were already seated inside, waving to loved ones from the windows. Tony turned around and took it all in—his grandfather's tears, his mother's sobbing, his father's solemn face, his sisters' smiles and waves, and Marco's taut stare as he tried to be strong for his only brother.

As the train whistled and started moving, Tony and Paul jumped on board.

* * * * *

In a large room, the nervous recruits stripped down and lined up to get their physicals and their typhoid and tetanus shots, while Sergeant Pearson moved all their civilian clothes into a pile for disposal. Though nobody spoke, Tony could feel the innocence of childhood seeping out of their skins as they faced a new reality.

"Cough," the doctor said, placing his stethoscope on Tony's chest.

Tony coughed, stuck out his tongue, did everything he was asked to do, and tried not to flinch as the doctor's cold hands examined him.

Outside, Sergeant Pearson marched the naked recruits across the grounds to the barracks. Nothing could be more demeaning. The simple life they had just left behind seemed a million miles away.

"I used to drive a Cadillac," Pearson sang in his booming baritone.

"I used to drive a Cadillac," the platoon echoed.

"Now I don't have the clothes on my back."

"Now I don't have the clothes on my back."

"My momma and daddy say I'm a hit."

"My momma and daddy say I'm a hit."

"The Army says I'm a piece of shit."

"The Army says I'm a piece of shit," the platoon yelled, as they came to a stop in front of the barracks.

Paul leaned into Tony and whispered, "Nothing like marching

with your dick hanging out." Everyone around them snickered at the remark.

"Shhh," Tony said, giving him the evil eye. The last thing he needed was to be chastised for talking out of turn.

But it was too late. Like a dog on high alert, Sergeant Pearson had heard the noise. He cocked his head and his eyes narrowed on Tony. *Shit! I'm going to kick his ass!*

"Hey, school-girl! Yeah, you with the dumb look on your face. Get over here!"

"Yes, sir!" He responded, double-timing it to the sergeant.

"Wipe that shit-eating grin off your face. This isn't summer camp!"

"No, sir! I mean, yes sir!" Tony replied, sticking his chest out so far that it hurt.

"An Okie?" the sergeant asked.

"No, sir!" he wondered what it was about him that made the sergeant figure he was a poor migrant worker from Oklahoma. He was clean and his hair was nicely trimmed.

"Well, you look like an Okie to me," the sergeant said, stepping forward until there was less than an inch between his face and torso and Tony's face and naked body.

"No, sir. I'm from California," Tony said, reflecting on the direction his life had taken in a few months. There he was, delivering Coca-Cola with his father, in love with Amy, and hoping that, with a little encouragement, their families would take to each other. Now, here he stood now, being examined and berated by his superior.

"Did I ask you where you were from?" The sergeant spat in his face.

"No, sir!" It was just a rite of passage, he told himself.

"You still look like an Okie to me. Okies are dumb, and have ears like jackasses," Pearson said, turning to an aide and asking, "You ever seen ears like that?"

"Only on my mule back home, sir."

Tony did not take it personally. He knew Pearson wanted to

toughen him up.

"Damn right. Those are Okie ears. Look straight! Don't look at me. Stand straight!"

"Yes, sir!"

"Drop down and give me twenty."

"Yes, sir!"

Tony dropped down and did a pushup. "One." He did a second pushup. "One! It doesn't count 'til your nuts must hit the ground!" the sergeant commanded, and Tony went lower on the next pushup. "Two."

It was going to be a long day.

* * * * *

The bare-skinned recruits stood before a long table to receive their uniforms and bedding. Army standard—two sheets, two blankets, one pillow case, two sets of fatigues, two pairs of boxer shorts, a pair of boots, and a chain with two dog tags. So much for style, Tony thought before getting dressed.

As the men made their bunks regulation style, Tony sneered at Paul. "Hey, dickhead, you owe me one."

"I was just trying to help, buddy. Just trying to help."

* * * * *

Outside, the new recruits stood at attention as Sergeant Pearson addressed them gruffly. "You are the most inept, slack-bellied bunch of girls I have ever seen. Listen good! You'll be heading out to fight the Japs. They're vicious, and those little bucktoothed bastards will chew you up and spit out the bones. You must be prepared, or they will slice you up seven ways from Sunday. They will go without food and water for days just for the chance to stick a knife in your gut. They're as hard and mean as a hungry tiger. And to deal with them, I've got *you*."

That "you" sounded like something disgusting on the sole of the sergeant's shoe. Tony wondered whether he got this characterization of the Japanese fighters from actual combat or from his colorful imagination.

"So we're gonna pound you into shape. You hear me?" The sergeant put his hands on his hips and roared, "You're gonna be soldiers when I get through with you, or you're gonna die trying. Right now, I'm not sure which I'd prefer, but it's gonna be one or the other! This little five mile run will separate the wheat from the chaff."

Five miles? He is he out of his mind! Tony was used to running ninety feet between bases, not five miles without any training.

The sergeant had two aides, corporals who looked every bit as mean as he did, and they led the column of men, singing as they ran. Bringing up the back of the pack, Tony wondered how come everyone else was in better shape than he was, when he lettered in baseball every year.

Boot camp was worse than he could have ever imagined. Both he and Paul ached in body parts they did not even know they had. Though they were not great starting material, every day they inched closer to their goals. The thought of one day seeing Amy again was the only thing that kept Tony going.

During rifle training, he discovered he was a good shot. With intensive coaching by the corporals, he became the best in his platoon. Every day, he held his rifle and marched with pride, and every night, in the few moments he had to himself before lights out, he wrote Amy a letter telling her how much he missed her.

* * * * *

Corporal Nagy was sorting the mail when he spotted a letter for that Amy bitch from that Italian kid back home. He sliced it open and scanned the letter: *Here at boot camp—, miss you more every day—, blah—, blah—, and more blah.*

What a whining, pathetic sap. I bet he has never touched her. He crumpled up the letter and threw it in the trash with dozens of other letters. *At least, that guinea should be thankful he's not stationed in this shithole.*

The quiet sound of shuffling feet made him look up, and there was the Japanese girl who had been coming around to flirt with him and then some. "Well, hello, Claire. Anything I can help you with today?" he asked in that tone he knew drove women crazy with delight.

Claire smiled the innocent smile that Nagy knew first-hand was not so innocent. "Do you have any letters for me?" she asked. *God, these Jap girls are so nobby with that whole innocence act.*

He rifled through the stack and found one belonging to her. "Why, I have it right here. But first, I require payment. You know, for the safe delivery of your letter." He grinned at her.

Her shy eyes cast a downward glance, and he could tell just by looking at her that she wanted that letter and wanted it bad. "Give me letter now, and I return at nighttime for longer time," she said shyly.

Nagy clucked his tongue. Now they were getting somewhere. "That's a deal," he said, handing her the letter, but just as she was about to take it with her delicate fingers, he pulled it back and leaned in, inhaling her scent. "Don't keep me waiting! You hear?"

"I won't," she said, batting her eyelashes. Slowly, she took the letter and bowed to him. She retreated to the back wall, opened the letter, and read it, savoring every last uncensored word from her fiancé who was imprisoned at the concentration camp in Heart Mountain, Wyoming.

Ring-a-ding-ding! Let's see. Tonight, I'll need a bottle of wine, a blanket, and don't forget johnnies.

A moment later, that Amy bitch and her little sisters walked in, acting like Dorothy and her gang trying to have a word with the Wizard of Oz. She was lucky she was still alive after what she did to him. She had some serious nerve coming around here.

"Well, if it isn't Amy Kashywaguy and her flunkies," Nagy said, making a sudden move for her, and Amy flinched. He laughed. She was still scared of him. *Perfect.* "What do you want?"

"I need to mail this." She handed him the unsealed letter.

He snatched it out of her hands, but she didn't leave. "What? Is there something else you want? Oh, let me guess. You want some more, right? And you brought your sisters because they want some too. Am I right?" Nagy laughed nastily, rubbing at his cheek, which bore a scar.

Her sisters turned to her for a clue as to what he was talking about, but Amy ignored them, keeping her eyes even with Nagy. "Is there any mail for me?"

He pressed a hand to his chest in mock surprise. "Oh. Don't you know? Your white GI has another girlfriend by now."

"GI? How do you know he's in the Army?"

"C'mon, every Joe in a uniform has been with you." He laughed at his own joke. *What is wrong with these people? No sense of humor.*

"Let's go," Amy said to June and Kelly.

"You need to take a lesson from Claire over there." Nagy nodded in Claire's direction.

Hearing her name, Claire looked up with tears streaming down her face. "Thank you for this," she said to Nagy, holding the letter out, as she headed for the door. "I'll be back later."

"You're very, very welcome, and I look forward to your visit, Claire." Nagy turned his eyes to Amy. "See? That girl knows how to get what she wants."

It's so easy for her, that bitch, to send and get her mail, but no, she insists on making life difficult. Well, that's just fine. If there's no quid, there's no quo.

When she and her sisters left, Nagy ripped Amy's letter in half, dropping the pieces into the same waste basket that held Tony's letter.

* * * * *

"Don't worry, Amy. He'll write when he can," June said, as the three sisters trudged back to their hovel. "Guys don't write as much as women do."

The girls walked by a bench where Mr. Fukuoka sat, bottle in hand, chatting with a friend. "Girls! Hi, girls!" he said, slurring his words. "Amy, June, Amy, where you are going?" He patted his buddy on the shoulder. "They nice. I lives with them."

"What're we, where are we going?" the buddy asked, standing up to greet them, but Amy felt nervous for her sisters and ushered them away.

"He's drinking again," June said, keeping her eyes down.

"Don't say anything, or Mrs. Fukuoka will worry." Amy warned, guiding her sisters onward.

* * * * *

Lying on their bunks, Tony opened just one letter, while Paul read several. As he slid it out of the envelope, it was not the letter he had been expecting or hoping for, but at least he had one. He sighed and read it to himself.

Paul looked over at him. "Your parents?"

"Yeah. Grandpa's out of the hospital."

"Tell them I said hi."

"I will. How's Debbie?" Tony asked with some trepidation. He was not sure he wanted to hear all about Paul's buxom blonde and the sweet, naughty things she was probably saying to him, but he did not want to be rude either.

Paul seemed to sense this. "Ah, you know how girls are. They go on and on," he replied. "Any word from Amy?"

Tony took a deep breath, folded his parents' letter, and set it aside. "Zilch."

"You will. I'm sure you will. It must be hard where she is."

Tony shrugged, trying to keep a brave face. "When she can write, I'll hear from her." He kept reminding himself how hard things must be for her, because she would never ignore him. He turned over in his bunk and closed his eyes.

* * * * *

With gray skies above them, Tony and Paul leaned against the ship's railing and stared out at the Pacific Ocean. Wind whistled around them and the waves crashed onto the bow. Whitecaps stretched as far as the eye could see, and the ship rocked underneath their feet. The two of them groaned, their stomachs under assault. "Wonderful. This is just wonderful," Paul said, as mists of sea-water spiked his face. "They train us to march, shoot and kill, and we spend all this time on a Goddamn ship, getting sick."

Tony held onto the railing. "Stop your crying. If our grandmothers made it to Ellis Island without bitching, you can handle this."

"Shut up," Paul said. "Hey, I saw that you got some mail. Did you hear from Amy?"

Tony shook his head. "It was from Marco. He French-kissed McDowell's little sister, and they beat Huntington Park."

"That kid is aces," Paul said, nodding. "Have you written to her lately?"

Tony did not know what was worse, the sea or Paul's questions. "I mailed another letter before leaving port. But I haven't heard a thing from her, if you must know." The thought that Paul knew how Amy was ignoring him irked him to no end. Then again, if he could not tell his best friend, who could he tell? He shrugged. "Maybe she forgot me. Maybe she blames me for everything. Ah, it's better this way." He turned so his back faced the sea.

"Don't give up, man. She wouldn't treat you like that on purpose. I'll have Debbie write to her and find out what's going on," Paul said, and they were quiet for a while. Tony longed for a change in topic, so when Paul spoke with a different voice tone, he was relieved. "Hey, Tony, after all our training, do you think you can get a man in your sights and pull the trigger? You know, will you be able to kill him?"

Tony now understood what was eating at Paul. It was the big question on all of their minds. After all, they were just kids only yesterday. "Don't worry. We're not gonna freeze up. It's nothing to be proud of, like some of the guys act, but we're gonna pull the trigger."

Chapter 20

Under the blazing New Guinea sun, General Hitoshi Imamura of the Eighth Area Army looked on as the sweat rolled off hundreds of bare chests. His men built pill boxes and concrete bunkers in the hills and laid land mines and barbed wire on the beaches. While they must not know of his concern, the bitter truth was he simply did not have enough soldiers or artillery. The Japanese High Command of the Imperial Army was confident of victory, but they were in Tokyo looking at maps and reading reports. Meanwhile, he was on an island that would soon be the target of American ships and infantry.

The politicians had overruled Admiral Isoroku Yamamoto. He had advised against war with the United States, arguing that Japan could "run wild" for six months to a year but then what? He had incurred the wrath of many members of the pro-war faction, and now there was a price on his head. The rumor was he was given command of the Navy to ensure his life.

But General Imamura held Admiral Yamamoto in the highest regard, and he realized that Japan was presently in the "then what?" stage of the war. The admiral had studied at Harvard and served as a naval attaché in Washington D.C. He had seen the immense industrial power of the United States. Now that giant was turning its manufacturing strength on them, churning out warships and planes in revenge. Nor did General Imamura believe his government's view that American soldiers were weak and soft. While his soldiers were superior, he had no doubt the Americans would train their soldiers to be formidable opponents. They would not turn and run when they hit the beaches.

General Imamura knew the battle of New Guinea would be won on the beach. If the Americans got a foothold, they would never be forced off the island. The only way to victory was to destroy them as soon as they touched the sand. He surveyed the beach one last time. The fighting would be savage, but he would prevail. The sand would run red with American blood. He was certain of it.

He stepped out of his Kurogane scout car, and his troops looked up. With complete confidence, he bellowed, "The enemy doesn't have a chance!"

His troops cheered, and in unison, they echoed, "The enemy doesn't have a chance."

General Imamura turned a palm toward the nearby dunes. "This beach will become a cemetery for our enemy!" The men raised their weapons in the air and shouted. He basked in their approval.

* * * * *

Mr. Kashiwagi entered the apartment more excited than Amy had seen since they were incarcerated. "They're starting a school," he told June and Kelly, and then he turned to his wife and Amy. "I've signed us up for jobs. We can work!"

"School?" Kelly whined. "But I don't like school."

"Anything is better than this," June said, jumping up from her seat and clapping.

Amy was not crazy about working, but she knew better than to disagree with her father. Besides, June was right. Anything was better than sitting around hoping this torture would end.

Amy was assigned to a second grade classroom as an assistant. In the cramped room, the students had to sit on the floor Indian-style—there were no desks, books, or supplies.

Mrs. Anderson, the second grade teacher, was a tall, stout American who welcomed Amy's help. "Welcome, class. My name is

Mrs. Anderson and my assistant is Amy Kashywaguy."

A student raised her hand.

"Yes?" the teacher asked.

"Her name is Amy Kashiwagi," the little girl solemnly informed Mrs. Anderson.

"Thank you. That's what I meant," the teacher replied somewhat sheepishly, and then she began the first lesson, reviewing the alphabet and all the long and short vowel sounds.

After school, the three sisters lumbered into the hovel. "What a gyp! We don't even have books," Kelly complained. "Worst school ever."

"Mom, we had to sit on the *floor*," June said. "And one of my teachers is a beautician. All she kept talking about was how to properly set rollers in your hair."

"Girls, it is just the first day," their mother said, as Amy changed her clothes. "Give it some time. It will get better."

* * * * *

While his wife took a job as a nurse at the camp hospital, where she worked alongside Mrs. Yamada, a dignified and proper lady, Mr. Kashiwagi took a job in the Manzanar warehouse, delivering food and supplies to the mess halls and collecting trash. It was several steps down from owning his own chain of corner grocery stores, but at least he had a purpose in life once more.

Corporals Lett and Duffy supervised Mr. Kashiwagi and his partner, Mars Sumida, a smart and curious detainee, as they loaded a truck with supplies. "You fishheads get your butts in gear. You got a full day ahead of you," Corporal Duffy ordered.

Fishheads! Have Mars and I been reduced to that?

"We got everything. Let's go," Mars said to Mr. Kashiwagi, as they climbed into the truck and set off along the camp's dirt roads, delivering food to the twelve mess halls in the prison. After their fourth delivery, Aito Morita, a volatile and energetic cook, pounded on the passenger door. "Do you have any sugar or coffee?"

"We're out," Mr. Kashiwagi replied.

"We can't be. We just received a shipment," Mars said.

"We're out," Mr. Kashiwagi reiterated, raising his eyebrows at Mars.

* * * * *

A shell exploded in the Coral Sea off the coast of New Guinea, splashing salt spray over the troops huddled in the Higgins landing craft. Tony and Paul exchanged ominous looks as yet another explosion rattled the boat and assaulted their eardrums. The boat swerved and tossed several soldiers from their standing positions.

Tony clutched his rifle with nervous anticipation as a shell hit a nearby landing craft and exploded, sending mangled body parts ricocheting through the air, He could smell everyone's fear.

Standing at the front of the landing craft, Sergeant Vogel barked, "Your mission is simple. Get your ass on shore. You hear me? Get your ass on shore!"

As they approached the beach, the boat slowed. Any second now, shots would be fired. If he was lucky, he would not get hit. It was that simple. Suddenly, the bottom of the boat hit ground and the ramp came down with a loud, metallic thud.

With a yell, the first soldiers charged out. Within seconds, Private John Lutz, a kid of eighteen, stumbled back with a softball-sized hole in his chest. He stared up at Tony for help, gasping for one more breath. Tony looked down at him and thought of the boy's family. But there was no time for compassion in his dying moment, as Vogel yelled, "Go, go, go!"

He jumped into the water, already teaming with corpses. Any moment now, it could all end. Making his way to shore, feeling the bullets whizzing past his helmet, Tony cursed the fate that had brought him here. To his right, Private Larry Weaver jerked back as a bullet caught him in the neck. In front of him, Private Kenneth Polaski dropped into the water, saturating the waves with blood. By some miracle, he reached the shore, finding Paul next to him, as they dove behind a small dune of grass and sand. Tony motioned for Private David Gilley to come and share their sacred spot, but as he ran a hail of bullets perforated his chest.

Tony burrowed deeper into the ground, his heart pounding wildly, but they could not wait here forever. It was a temporary shelter at best. They had to move fast. "Are you ready?" he asked Paul, whose hands shook so badly that he could barely hold up his rifle.

Paul nodded, briefly meeting his eyes. There, behind his utter terror, hid the wise-cracking friend he had cherished since the first day of kindergarten, the man with whom he shared his darkest fears and his greatest desires.

Tony and Paul raised their guns and fired, drawing a slew of bullets. They lowered down, and Tony prayed to God and all the saints to please keep them alive. Peering around, he caught sight of a taller ridge and knew it was their only hope. He slapped Paul on the shoulder and pointed. "Let's get there, on three. One, two—"

Chapter 21

The door to their cell opened, and in her nurse's uniform, Mrs. Kashiwagi entered, all flummoxed. "Girls, put on something nice. We're eating with the Yamadas. They have sons your age. Let's go, no time to waste."

After a full day with second graders, Amy just wanted to lie in bed and read *The Yearling* for the eighth time. "Do we have to?" she groaned, knowing her mother wanted to match her up with a boy.

"Get dressed. It's good to meet new people," her mother said in that tone Amy usually did not mess with. While it was true her mother's plans and hers had not exactly coincided with each other lately, Amy was turning twenty in two months, and she was ready to be on her own, as much as one could be on one's own in a concentration camp. Besides, she still had not given up on Tony, though she often thought she should.

"I can't. I have papers to grade," Amy said, without looking up. She pulled a stack of papers out of her bag, along with a red pen, to show how busy she was.

"You can do them after dinner. I said get dressed." Her mother glared at her, and though Amy felt a small fire growing in her chest, she did as her mother requested. There was no point in getting into an argument with her when she had to eat supper anyway.

At the mess hall, the Yamadas, dressed in kimonos, were waiting for them. Mr. and Mrs. Yamada and their sons, Hiroto and Isamu, greeted the Kashiwagis with a bow, and Mr. and Mrs.

Kashiwagi bowed back. Amy wondered why her parents were going back to the old ways. She rolled her eyes at Kelly. Neither she nor her sisters bowed. Americans did not bow, and they were Americans.

Amy was sure Hiroto and Isamu were nice young men, but she was not interested. She only wanted to see a letter from Tony, so this whole meal and its hidden agenda was a waste of time.

At dinner, Hiroto, the elder of the two brothers, tried to demonstrate how to use chopsticks, but Amy and her sisters were unresponsive. Hiroto shrugged his shoulders and said, "I don't mind if you use them or not, but our parents believe we should keep the old customs. They have never accepted American ways." He gestured around the dirty building. "And this may well prove them right."

Amy was about to give a polite reply about how American ways were not like this, how maybe if Japan had not attacked them, none of this would have happened, when the door to the mess hall opened and Mr. Fukuoka stumbled in. "Hi, Mr. Fukuoka," Kelly said, waving to her housemate. He staggered over and fell onto the table, sending food flying everywhere.

"I do apologize," Mrs. Kashiwagi said, rushing over to help him. "This place has crushed him."

"He used to be somebody," Mr. Kashiwagi added, helping Mr. Fukuoka to stand on his own feet.

"Didn't we all," Mr. Yamada lamented.

* * * * *

Hearing the spatter of machine gun fire, Tony and Paul dove into a bomb crater that was still smoldering. Tony caught a glimpse of the machine gun nest—two Japanese gunners, one feeding the gun, one shooting. He patted Paul on the back and pointed to it. Paul signaled the others, and at his nod, Private Floyd Heaton and Private Harold Mathauer rose up and fired at the nest. While their bullets hit wood and dirt, Tony and Paul used the distraction to scramble to a closer crater.

Paul held out a grenade for him. "Sling this down the strike zone. I'll cover you."

Pulling out the pin, Tony threw the grenade, while Paul fired. The blast lifted one of the Japanese soldiers, minus an arm, then slammed him back into the dirt. The second soldier was spun around by the blast, blood and flesh sent spinning through the air.

They raced toward the nest, rifles firing, finishing-off the two Japanese machine gunners. A third Japanese solider retreated, firing as he left. Paul fired two shots, catching him in the chest, and he slumped to the ground. They dashed behind some palm trees and caught their breath.

"Anybody hurt?" Tony yelled.

"No," Heaton responded.

"Just those guys," Private Michael Fugett said.

"Let's keep it that way, Tony said, scanning the landscape. His gaze landed on a blown up bunker. "Concrete box up ahead. Let's go for it!"

Bullets whizzed past them. Tony dove into the empty bunker with Paul and Heaton and Mathauer followed them.

* * * * *

Catching up to her father in the biting wind, Amy asked, "Dad, can I walk with you?" She was not sure what she wanted to tell him, considering they never talked about anything important, but maybe just being with him would soothe her mind after a busy day at school.

"Yes, of course, sweetheart," he said, stopping and staring at her as if for the first time.

They walked to a dark corner of the camp and met up with Aito and Mars, who used a pair of field glasses to watch a group of men outside the camp warehouse. "What are they doing?" Amy asked her father.

"The rats are in action," Mars said. Amy was not sure what that meant.

Although the lights were dim, Amy could make out the men moving around, creating shadows against the walls and fences. They were loading crates on a truck.

"Lett and Duffy are taking sugar, coffee and cigarettes," Aito said, peering through the binoculars. "I knew it—the black market. Hell, I bet coffee brings a high price!"

Another soldier, carrying a box, walked into the light. "Who's that?" Mr. Kashiwagi asked, crouching low.

"Don't know," Aito mumbled.

Amy gasped. Even from this distance, she would recognize that profile anywhere. "It's Nagy, from the post office."

"You sure?" her father asked.

"Here, give me those," she said. Aito handed the field glasses to her. She looked through the lenses and saw the hulking figure of the man who had attacked her nineteen months before. She would never forget that form as long as she lived. "It's him all right."

"No wonder the mail is so screwy," Aito scoffed. "My parents have only received a third of my letters."

A fourth man came out of the building. Amy stiffened when she saw him. As she watched, he handed a stack of cash to the other men, then climbed into the driver's seat of the truck. "That's— that's the son of— that's Jeff Schultz," she spluttered in amazement, remembering long forgotten days in the store, the way things used to be.

"Who?" Aito asked.

Schultz started the truck and drove off.

"Dad, that guy was Mr. Schultz's son, Jeff. I'm sure of it."

Dumbstruck, Mr. Kashiwagi stared back at his daughter.

* * * * *

In their foxhole, Tony allowed himself to close his bloodshot eyes for a few precious moments. He opened them to find Paul pulling a battered pack of cigarettes from his breast pocket. He offered one to

Tony. Even though he had never been one to smoke, he took it and stuck it in his mouth.

Paul flicked his lighter. Tony steadied his hand, helping him light both cigarettes.

"Thanks," Paul said.

"You gotta calm the hell down," Tony mumbled.

"Hell! I never imagined I'd spend my twentieth birthday in this shithole."

"Really? Today is fifteenth?" He had forgotten. In the moonlight, Paul nodded. "Well, Happy Birthday!" Tony clapped him on the shoulder, remembering when Paul turned seventeen and they got sick on that pint of whiskey.

"Thanks man."

They were so accustomed to the sounds of artillery fire by now that they did not even look up when bombs blasted in the distance, creating a flare of light which soon faded in the night sky. "I guess they're not gonna surrender," Paul said, breaking Tony's train of thought.

"Not those bastards. Didn't you listen to the lectures? Or were you catching some shut-eye?"

"I heard 'em." Paul puffed on his cigarette. The tip glowed orange in the darkness. "It just doesn't make sense. They can't win, not this battle anyway."

Tony shook his head. "Doesn't matter; to the last man. That's their philosophy."

"I just don't understand it." Their eyes met, and Tony saw the fear in Paul's eyes.

"Maybe it's the Crazy Eddie Rule," Tony said.

The memory drew Paul out, and his hand stopped shaking. "God! Crazy Eddie and Nicky. What a pair! Nicky would beat the shit out of him, and Eddie would yell, 'Fuck you!'"

"He didn't get a full deck, but you've got to admit, he was funny as hell!" Tony said. They laughed. It felt good to laugh, so much that he and Paul fell into a fit of it—crazy laughter, the kind that was bred from stress.

"I've got to piss," Tony said, drawing on his cigarette to calm down. He got up and stumbled behind a tree.

"How many did we lose in that banzai attack?" Paul asked.

"Floyd for one. He had two kids. Michael too," Tony answered, thinking about their wives and children, what they would go through once they received the news.

"Yeah, I'm gonna write his parents," Paul said. "He was from Weyauwega, Wisconsin. Can you believe Weyauwega, Wisconsin? No wonder he was such a funny bastard. You'd have to be if you came from Weyauwega, Wisconsin."

"He was a helluva guy," Tony said, zipping up. He came around the tree and sat back down. "I can't write anymore. All those letters to that bitch and not one reply." Tony shook his head. He was surprised to hear himself use that word to describe Amy, but then again, he had not realized how angry he was with her until now.

"Don't say that. Maybe her parents are getting 'em. You know how they hated you. They're stickin' their nose where it doesn't belong. That's all it is, Tony."

"Screw that. That shouldn't stop her from writing. I got the kiss-off." Tony looked up, spying the next line of resistance. "We better get some sleep. It'll be light out in a couple of hours."

Chapter 22

A warm body filled every chair in the mess hall for the Japanese Council of Manzanar meeting, and at least fifty people stood along the back and side walls as Mr. Kashiwagi, Mars, Aito, and Amy addressed their fellow detainees from the front of the room. "For three months, we've observed four GIs stealing from us," Mars declared.

"Three council members saw it too," Mr. Kashiwagi echoed.

An elderly Japanese man stood up. The crowd, which had been murmuring, quieted. Mr. Teryuki, the residents' unofficial ambassador to the commander, was well-respected at Manzanar. "Perhaps before we act, we should know all the details."

Mr. Kashiwagi nodded. "Several nights ago, we observed Corporals Nagy, Lett, and Duffy loading crates of sugar, coffee and cigarettes onto a truck. Another soldier paid them, then drove off in the truck. Whenever the camp receives a shipment of goods, a few days later, we see them loading those goods onto a truck in the middle of the night."

"We suspected this was going on," said a woman in the audience. "There are always shortages. The obvious answer is someone is stealing."

"Let's take action!" shouted Hiro Matsuda, who was never the most sensible person in the camp with his fiery temper. He raised his fist. "First they steal our homes and businesses, then they lock us up in this prison. Now they steal from us again. I say we don't take it anymore. Let's march and demand justice!"

Several other men stood up and yelled their agreement. "We've suffered enough! The time to stand and fight is now."

"But they won't listen to us. We have no rights here," a woman said, her thin voice rising above the menfolk.

"We have nothing left to lose," another man replied.

Amy agreed with him. As a victim of the abuse, she was tired of it all. *What can they do for voicing their displeasure, imprison them?*

Mr. Teryuki raised his hands to quiet the room. It took several minutes but finally the yells and shouts diminished. "Fighting is suicidal," he said calmly. "We must go to the camp commander and tell him what is going on. He will put a stop to it."

"What if he doesn't?" someone asked.

"He's probably in on it." Hiro spoke above the crowd. "And how come you always take their side? Are you in on it too?"

"Please, let's be rational," Mr. Teryuki said, holding out his hands, but most of the crowd agreed with the impassioned young man.

"He can't be a good commander if his men steal from under his nose," someone said.

"Hell, he's getting his cut," one young man yelled. "They all are."

Others jumped up and said, "He's right. He's in on it."

"Thieves won't stop other thieves. It's up to us to stop them!" Someone else shouted.

Throughout it all, Mr. Kashiwagi sat, absorbing it all. Amy watched him, wondering what he was thinking. Would he ever choose a side? He could not possibly be on both. Diplomacy was not possible anymore. Either he was Japanese or he was American, and look at what America had done to them.

"No! This is not the way!" Mr. Teryuki yelled. "Please, everyone, sit down!"

"It's the only way!" Shouted a voice in the crowd. "Come on!"

To Amy's horror, dozens of people stormed out and headed for the commander's office, brandishing bottles from the trash bins, clubs, and rocks.

Sirens went off. Soldiers clenched their weapons. The protestors yelled in Japanese, rioting toward the commander's office. Rocks and bottles flew everywhere, breaking windows.

"Dad, what do we do?" Amy asked, but her father looked around, doing nothing. Amy wanted to shake him to get him to move.

Guards appeared from every direction, as if they had been tipped off, lining up in front of the commander's office. Other soldiers, weapons in hand, surrounded the angry mob. An explosion rocked the night, and flames flared from the windows of a storage shed. The guards aimed their rifles at the crowd and a shot rang out.

"Oh, my God!" Amy screamed.

Another guard flinched, firing two more shots.

"Dad, let's go," Amy pleaded, as her father slipped and fell. She helped him up, and he limped home with her assistance.

"That was terrible, just terrible," he said. "What is happening to us?"

Inside their cell, more gunfire was heard. "Are you okay?" Amy asked, as she eased her father down in a chair.

"I am just sore," he said. "We never should have called the meeting. They were already angry enough."

"Who knew—" Another gunshot rang out. Amy looked toward the door. "I'm going—"

"Stay here!" he ordered. The urgency in her father's voice stopped her, and she slowly sank into the chair next to him.

Sometime later, they heard a knock on the door. Amy ran over and opened it, letting Mars into their hovel. "What happened?" she asked, seeing the distress in his eyes.

"Aito and four others are dead."

* * * * *

Throughout the day, fewer and fewer Japanese guns sounded. Their positions were being chewed up by American fire. While artillery shells flew overhead, Tony crawled toward the Japanese position.

Suddenly a mortar exploded twenty feet from him, showering him with dirt and fragments of shrapnel. A piece cut into his face; he could feel the heat and his blood trickling down his cheek. As he looked around, he slapped his ears in frustration. His world had gone silent. "I can't hear!" he yelled.

Paul turned to him. His lips moved, but Tony did not hear a word. He scanned his other friends' lips in a panic and heard nothing, just an incessant ringing in his ears.

Scouting the terrain ahead, Paul gestured to a crater that could serve as shelter from enemy fire overhead. Tony understood what to do. Paul raised one finger, a second finger, and on three they raced for the cavity while machine gun fire spat bullets around their feet. Miraculously, they made it.

Once he was down, the ringing in Tony's ears lessened, and little by little, he began to hear the firing outside. "That was hell," he said, realizing how valuable his ears were in battle.

"You can hear?" Paul asked.

"Yeah. I'm okay."

Paul leaned back on the crater wall. "That's two more packs you owe me."

Out of the corner of his eye, Tony spotted a Japanese soldier who fired from the edge of the hole. Paul only had time to groan as the bullet pierced his eye and he sagged, slowly to the ground. Tony fired twice. Both bullets hit the Jap's stomach as he fell into the crater, gurgling in pain.

Tony turned toward his best friend, but it was too late. An empty eye-socket stared back at him, leaking blood. "Paulie," he howled, shaking him. "Look at me!"

But the light in Paul's face had already died away.

The Japanese soldier mouthed some words. It was nothing defiant or prayer-like; more like a plead for help. Tony raised his rifle. "Yeah? What about Paul? Who's gonna help him?" He fired until the chamber was empty, shattering the man's face, wiping out his nose, his eyes, and all of his brains. "There's your fucking help!"

He dropped his weapon and sobbed.

Chapter 23

Tony walked under the "Welcome Home Soldiers" banner that stretched across the pier. A nice touch, he thought, setting foot on Hawaii along with hundreds of other soldiers for a well-deserved rest and recuperation break. He was twenty pounds lighter than his induction weight, but he had matured beyond his years. Now every step had a purpose.

Entering a grocery store for a pack of Chesterfields and a bottle of Coca-Cola, Tony noticed the gold star displayed in the front window. Feeling strangely hollow, he imagined the Romanos had an identical one in their living room window to honor Paul's memory. Grabbing a Coke out of the cooler, he stared at the bottle. It felt like forever and a day since he had worked with his dad.

He snagged a pack of smokes, and at the counter, two Japanese kids did their homework.

Smiling, the owner walked over to the cash register. "Anything else?"

"You Japanese?" Tony asked.

The man nodded, unsure, it seemed, as to what judgment Tony was about to bestow upon him.

"How come you're not in a camp?" Tony asked, lighting a cigarette.

"No need. Everyone is for the United States."

"Ain't that the truth." Tony glanced down at the boy and girl who were not more than five or six years old. "They yours?"

"My grandkids. My son died at Pearl Harbor."

Tony tipped his hat. "I'm sorry to hear that. They're good-looking kids."

"Thanks. They're a joy to have. I'm Haruo Suzuki. Most people call me Harry."

"Mr. Suzuki, Tony Piccinin." Tony shook the storeowner's hand, then leaned over and examined the boy's homework. "Your sister needs to help you. Five plus three doesn't equal six." The little girl, who was younger than her brother, looked up at him, smiling.

As Tony was talking, two GIs entered. "Hey Jap, two Cokes. Chop, chop!" one said, laughing at his own joke, as if it was the funniest thing ever uttered.

The boy turned his head to him. "Eight."

The soldier repeated himself. "Chop, chop! Get it?" The second soldier laughed.

"You sure?" Tony straightened up and glared at the two enlisted men. They remained oblivious to his stare.

"Yes."

"You're right." Tony ruffled the boy's hair.

Mr. Suzuki opened two Cokes from the cooler and set them on the counter.

"You Japs should be locked up," the first GI sneered.

Tony took a step forward, but Mr. Suzuki gently put his hand on his arm.

The first GI gave Tony a cold, confused stare. Tony prepared himself for any comments that might come his way, but they tossed two nickels on the counter and strutted out.

Once the door closed, Tony let his guard down. "Mr. Suzuki, why'd you let them talk to you like that? I'd have—"

"What? Start a fight?" The man's dark eyes narrowed at Tony.

"They'd understand that."

"What if they smashed the place up, hurt you, me, the children, then what?"

"Yeah, but—"

"Anger is not the way. Sometimes it is best to let things go. Look around you. They're gone, but we're still here." Mr. Suzuki handed him his drink. "On me."

"I can't." Tony put too many coins on the counter for the drink and the cigarettes. "You take care." With a heavy heart, he left.

A slight breeze blew across Tony's forehead as he headed down the street. The sky was an incredible marine blue. It was a beautiful, tranquil day, in sharp contrast to the horrors he had seen on an island not so long ago.

Across the street he watched as several Japanese people strolled by. *This doesn't make sense. President Roosevelt imprisoned the Japanese in California but not here in Hawaii, where it all started. How can they be a security risk in the states, but not in Hawaii? God, I bet it's politics—that's all it is!*

Sipping his soda, he was pleasantly surprised as two couples walked toward him—two white men holding hands with two Japanese women. They smiled at him as they passed. He thought of Amy, and a tear welled in his eye.

This is as it should be—couples in love under a sunny sky— God's perfection. But reality was blood and death on New Guinea and a concentration camp in California holding his love captive, while.

* * * * *

Mr. Kashiwagi and Mars loaded a truck under the watchful eye of new soldiers sent in after the riot. They couldn't help but notice that while others regarded them with scorn, two guards smiled and nodded as they worked. One even helped them load the truck.

"What did you hear about the others?" Mr. Kashiwagi asked Mars, as they leaned on the truck to rest a moment.

"Transferred with promotions. Can you believe it? The board said they were due for promotions! What's worse, the record showed each one had over forty thousand in the bank on a hundred and ten a month. Now, that's some justice," Mars mocked.

Mr. Kashiwagi shrugged. "Maybe this bunch will be better."

"It's a thin reed, but we can hope."

* * * * *

After running the mountains of Hawaii with a full backpack, Tony entered the barracks, dripping sweat. Tubby, a stray cat that the men had taken in, lay purring on his bunk, while hung-over men snored all around him.

"C'mon, Tubby, up and at 'em." Tony pushed the stubborn cat, but he refused to move.

A sleepy soldier got up and popped two aspirin. He blinked at Tony. "How far?"

"Eight."

"Just eight? You're letting us down! You should come out for once. Tommy Dorsey is playing tonight."

"He is?"

* * * * *

With two companions, Tony sauntered over to the USO hall.

"Tony, what's your line?" Bill asked.

"What?"

Jem interjected, "You know. Like, 'I'm new in town. Can you give me directions to your place?' Or, 'Hey, I recognize you. You're in all the magazines!'"

Tony had never used a line before. He saw them as a crutch, a replacement for a real personality. He had never needed them with Amy.

The three of them passed two Japanese prostitutes wearing dresses that showed too much leg. "You're some fine-looking men," one of the women said.

"I'll say. I like the blond one," her partner said, giving Jem a flirty smile.

"Does anyone need a date?" the first prostitute asked.

149

"If I don't get a skirt inside, I'll be back," Bill replied.

"Honey, why fish when you got a sure thing?"

"See? There's a line!" Jem said, laughing at his buddy.

"Never underestimate the power of a good line," Bill agreed.

"You notice— the prostitutes are all Japanese?" Tony asked.

"Of course. They have skills the white girls don't!" Bill elbowed him.

Inside the USO hall, the Tommy Dorsey Orchestra played to a packed room. Two dozen couples danced on the floor, some better than others. More than one woman gave a yelp, as her foot was stepped on. A slender brunette with brown eyes walked up to Tony, showing a shy smile, as his two friends looked on with envy. "I haven't seen you before."

"You sure? I'm in all the magazines," Tony said, forcing a laugh. "Sorry, that was lame."

"Yeah. That one just lay there. I'm Julietta Barzini." She held out her hand.

"I can match it. I'm Antonio Niccolo Piccinin," he said, shaking her hand gently. She had soft, delicate hands. "But everyone calls me Tony."

"Well, Tony will you be a sport and cut a groove with me?"

"Eh, I'm a little rusty," he said.

He had not danced in two years, since that fateful evening with Amy.

"C'mon, don't be an egg." She grabbed his hand and led him onto the dance floor. He may not have danced in a long time but soon it all came back to him, and he even performed a few of his signature moves. Julietta kept up just fine. Several other couples slowed down just to watch them.

"You're *rusty?*" She gave him a wary eye.

Tony smiled. "You're the dancer. I'm just following your lead."

They twirled a few more times before the music ended and everyone broke into wild applause.

After forty-five minutes of dancing, they sat down for a

cigarette and a couple of beers. Julietta inched closer. "I have to work tomorrow. Can you—"

"I'd love to—" Tony said, without thinking.

"What?" she asked, with her eyebrows raised.

"Walk you home," he clarified.

"Are you a mind reader?"

"That and a few other things." Tony smiled.

Her parents' home was a small, white-trimmed house. A solitary light on the front porch was on. They stood and smiled at each other. "Will I see you again?" she asked.

"Julietta, I don't want to chisel—"

"Don't tell me. You're rationed."

"I am. At least I think I am."

She paused for a moment. "You haven't heard from her for a while."

"How'd you know?"

"I'm a mind reader, too," she said, slinking up to him. As she slid up his chest and planted a soft kiss on his lips, Tony felt a stirring he hadn't experienced in a long time. "If you ever need a pal, I'm here for you."

Now that was a line, and then some.

Chapter 24

Amy finished her letter to Tony. *"I hope this letter finds you well. Daily I pray for your safety. I miss you more and more every day. With love, Amy."*

She followed her usual route to the post office. When she entered, she handed the letter to the new clerk, Corporal Lockhart. "Please wait," he said, scanning her letter for anything that might compromise the war effort.

Amy appreciated the kindness in his tone.

"This is fine," he said, sealing the envelope.

* * * * *

Someone had left the letter on his bunk. He patted Tubby. "Hey, buddy, who's this letter from, huh?"

The cat meowed as Tony opened the envelope. He read the letter from his parents and slammed his hand on the bunk, causing an anxious meow from Tubby.

His mother wrote: *Tony, thankfully, your grandfather suffered very little during his last days. He did get weaker as time went on but he was in very little, if any, pain. Toward the end, there was a definite twinkle in his eye. But like a flame on a candle, his life just flickered out. We were all blessed by his warmth and love. He did want you to know he loved you and was very proud of you. He constantly told his friends that his grandson was serving in the United States Army. Father Carlotto conducted the funeral. It was very dignified. You know how your grandfather liked wide, open spaces. We buried him out in the country at Forest*

Lawn Cemetery.

Tony swallowed again, holding down his tears. It was all too much—first Paul, and now his grandfather. He wished he had been there to say goodbye to him. Damn wars, he thought. Damn all of them.

His mother also had good news. He perked up at her cheerful words. *Maybe they had heard from Amy?* Tony turned the page and read on. Bruno had proposed to Angela on July 4th. They would be getting married before he entered the Army. *My sister! I thought he had more sense than that.*

Tony flung the letter into the trash.

* * * * *

The buzz at Honolulu Stadium was palpable, with most people talking about the Yankee Clipper. They had never expected to see the great Joe DiMaggio play in person. He had enlisted, but his superiors had insisted he play exhibition baseball in an effort to boost morale in the armed forces and among the civilians.

Tony and Julietta bumped and jostled other fans as they made their way through the turnstiles and stopped at the concession stand, buying hot dogs and sodas. "Wonder if he'll steal home?" one man asked as he strolled by with a friend.

"Only if he gets on third base. But that's doubtful because he'll probably hit a home run."

In a sea of soldiers and civilians, Tony and Julietta found their seats. He was in his element, and the crowd was cheerful and ready for the game to start. "In forty-one, American League MVP, should it have been DiMaggio or Williams?" Julietta asked. The question was music to his ears.

"That's tough," Tony said. "DiMaggio gets a hit in fifty-six straight games, and Williams bats four-o-six. It's impossible. It should've been co-MVPs. You?"

"DiMaggio, of course." Her brown curls bounced on her

slender shoulders.

"Why?" Tony asked.

"He's better looking." She smiled.

Tony laughed, intentionally bumping her with his shoulder. "And I thought you were sensible."

Julietta winked. "C'mon. It's the only way to solve the dilemma."

"Yes, I'm sure the sports writers gave that due consideration when they cast their ballots." He took a bite of his hot dog.

The Honolulu Sharks were playing the California Redwoods, DiMaggio's team. The Redwoods' lead-off batter singled sharply to right field, to the cheers of the crowd. But the second batter struck out, and the third flew out to short center field. DiMaggio was hitting clean-up. When he stepped into the batter's box, the crowd roared. He acknowledged the applause with a tip of his hat, then turned to face the pitcher.

Julietta reached over and held Tony's hand. He smiled. As much as he wished it were Amy's hand touching his, it was nice to feel close to a girl again.

"Strike!" the umpire called, as the fast ball popped into the catcher's mitt.

DiMaggio took an easy practice swing. The pitcher stared at the catcher to get the sign. He wound up and threw a slider. DiMaggio tensed, then eased as the ball curved outside the strike zone.

After getting the sign, the pitcher nodded. Again, he wound up and unleashed a fast ball, but DiMaggio was faster. He swung, and the whole stadium heard the crack of his bat against the ball. The crowd erupted to their feet, applauding wildly, with whistles and shouts, as Joe rounded the bases.

Tony turned to Julietta. "That was aces!"

"Yeah, we can tell our kids someday that we saw the great Joe DiMaggio hit a homer! Not many baseball fans can say that." Julietta smiled at him.

Tony returned the smile but said nothing. In truth, he was

completely taken aback by her statement. This was only their first date, and as much as he hated to admit it, the prospect of replacing Amy was much harder than he had anticipated.

Even after DiMaggio's homer, the Sharks fought back. They were a fast team and, when several players hit singles, one base runner stole third, another stole second, and their teammates batted them in. In the bottom of the ninth inning, the Redwoods led five to four. With two men on base and two outs, the Sharks' right fielder knocked the cover off the ball. It zoomed toward center. DiMaggio raced toward the wall. At the last split-second he leaped and the ball smacked into his glove.

Tony jumped up and cheered with glee, as did Julietta. They were so happy, they hugged, and the time just felt right. The embrace turned into a long, sweet kiss. And actually, Tony did not mind, not one little bit.

After the game, Joe DiMaggio wore his Army uniform and signed autographs for everyone. After the last fan left, Tony and Julietta approached him. "Joe, do you have a second?" Tony asked.

"I always have time for a soldier. What can I sign for you?"

"I just want to introduce myself. I'm Tony, and this is Julietta. I believe you knew my grandfather and mom."

"Who's that?"

"Roberto and Maria Sansone," Tony said.

DiMaggio's face lit up. "I don't just know them. They were like a second family to me on North Beach. How are they?"

"I thought you might have heard, but Grandpa died about a month ago. I'm sure my mom wrote your parents."

"I'm sorry to hear that," DiMaggio replied. "I haven't heard from my folks in a while. How's your mom?"

"She's fine," Tony replied. He could not believe he was talking to DiMaggio. *Joe DiMaggio!* As soon as he got back to the barracks, he would write Marco and tell him.

"Please pass on my condolences. I'll never forget your grandparents. Your grandfather loved baseball, and your grandmother was a helluva cook. I ate there as often as I could. I'll never forget the day she died in that accident. What a shame."

All too soon, Joe had to leave. As Tony and Julietta strolled back to town, Julietta asked, "How did your grandmother die?"

"I don't know. I heard Joe say accident, but I always thought it was cancer or something. I know my mother had two brothers who died of whooping cough, and when her mom died, she and my grandpa moved down to Los Angeles. Then she met my father. That's all I know." Tony thought for several seconds. "But now, things make more sense."

"Like what?" Julietta asked.

"My mom crowds you—always worried, nervous about everything. She can't relax. I'm sure it goes back to that."

* * * * *

"Tony Piccinin," the mail clerk called.

A short young man with curly brown hair stepped forward to receive the letter. Reading the return address, he grimaced in disappointment. "This isn't mine. I don't know an Amy Kashywaguy in Manzanar, California. I'm from New York."

"I'll take it," the clerk said, examining the envelope— Manzanar, California. A light bulb went on in his head. That was where the Army imprisoned the Japs. Thinking some Jap broad wanted money from some poor sap, he tossed the letter in the trash.

Chapter 25

"I'm sorry there's no letter," Corporal Lockhart said with a sympathetic look. "The mail isn't always prompt. Letters can be delayed for weeks and even months on account of the war. You know that, don't you?"

"I understand." Amy nodded, appreciating his helpful demeanor, whether or not it was true that her letter was delayed. At least she was not dealing with Corporal Nagy.

"Is the letter from a soldier?" he asked.

"Yes, I thought we had something special."

"I'm sure you do. Where's he stationed?"

"In the Pacific," she said, fighting back tears. "That's all I know. I've never heard from him. I don't know if he is dead or alive." Her anguish was too much to bear, and Amy made no attempt to hide her tears.

"Don't give up. He's alive. I know it." His kind voice soothed her.

"Thank you." She wiped away her eyes and headed outside, where she bumped into Hiroto from their ill-fated dinner. He was about to mail a package. In a shirt and jeans, he looked quite different and far more approachable than in his kimono.

He recognized her with a smile. "Amy, I want to apologize for what happened. My parents are fuddy-duddies. There was nothing I could do."

"That's okay. Sometimes traditional is good."

"It is, but with my parents, it's all the time. By the way, *Yankee*

Doodle Dandy is playing in the mess hall on Friday. Would you like to go?"

"Wow, you act fast!"

Hiroto blushed then regained his composure. "I just want a second chance with the most beautiful girl in camp. That's all. I promise things will be better this time."

"Ah, that's sweet. You must pardon me. I'm just not myself lately." Amy paused, thinking, just maybe, Tony's letter was on its way to her. Then she sighed, knowing it was not. She smiled at Hiroto. "Actually, going to a movie would be nice."

* * * * *

Tony stopped in for a Coke and to help the two Suzuki kids with their homework before meeting up with Nancy after work. They were intelligent and caught on quickly. Leaving them with some math problems, he went over to talk to Mr. Suzuki. They had become good friends over the last few weeks, and during their many conversations Tony had told him all about Amy. From the look on his face, Mr. Suzuki guessed Tony wanted to revisit the subject.

"Still no letter?" the storeowner asked.

"Mr. Suzuki, it's been over two years. I feel like such a sap."

"No, you are very faithful. That's a good trait."

"I don't know. It seems—"

Mr. Suzuki tapped his chest. "What do you think about Amy, in here?"

Tony did not answer immediately. "I just don't know anymore."

* * * * *

Under the light of a full moon, Hiroto and Amy strolled through the prison. The moon's reflection caressed Amy's face, and Hiroto thought it magnified her beauty in this most desolate place. "I had a good time," he said.

"So did I. That James Cagney is something else." She smiled at him. "Thank you for inviting me."

"My pleasure," he said, as they reached her cell.

"Will I see you again?" Amy asked with a pleasant upturn of her chin, her expression reminiscent of a Japanese Hakata doll.

"Of course," he said, putting his hands around her waist and pulling her close. Amy tilted her head and closed her eyes, and Hiroto kissed her.

* * * * *

The next weeks passed in a whirlwind for Tony and Julietta. They spent all of their free time together, watching movies, cycling and walking in the parks and along the beach, and eating at Honolulu's finest restaurants, where servicemen were treated like royalty. One night, they even had dinner with her parents, who seemed to approve of their daughter's new beau.

After an evening together, Tony's excitement about his new girlfriend prompted him to write his parents. "*I am seeing someone special. Her name is Julietta Ysabel Barzini, and yes, she's one hundred percent Northern Italian. Her father is a Naval Intelligence Officer. He was transferred here from San Diego after the attack on Pearl Harbor. Julietta works on the base as a secretary. We first met at a USO dance where she volunteers. She's a real good dancer. Tell Dad that the Tommy Dorsey Orchestra played at the dance. I met her parents. They were swell. You two would like her. Last night we even talked about our plans for after the war. She might be the one.*"

He sat back and reread what he had written. At those last words, a spike of guilt shot through his mind. Was Julietta really the one? His parents would appreciate hearing that, that was for sure. But as he read the last sentence again, he sighed.

Julietta was attractive, fun to be around, friendly, and she had no bad traits as far as he could tell. There was nothing wrong with her, and everything felt right. While every man and every woman had idiosyncrasies—hell, his parents had lots of them, and even he had a

159

few—she had none that really bothered him.

Amy! Her name popped into his mind and he dropped his pen on the table. If he was truly falling in love with one girl, surely he should not still be thinking of the last one. Maybe it was irrational, but whenever he thought of her, even now, his heart skipped a beat, recalling her laughter, her smile, and her manner; even something as innocuous as the way she said hello to strangers.

Sighing, Tony realized that when he thought of Julietta, his heart did not skip a beat. It simply continued its monotonous drumming, the same way it would if he had thought of any other girl. Maybe he needed to spend more time with her. Maybe she was too *new.*

His mind was racing. If he compared the two girls objectively, they would get the same ranking. Both were intelligent, attractive, and neither one yelled or nagged. He had seen flashes of temper from Julietta at times, but they were kept under control. Amy did not have a temper at all, and she possessed ample portions of basic humanity, a grace and gentleness toward others that was admirable.

But, if she is so kind and noble, why hasn't she written? If she wants to give me the kiss-off, why doesn't she tell me? Why does she leave me hanging?

He pushed back on the chair. It was not like her to walk away without another word. She had her integrity. If she were going to kick him to the curb, she would have written and been as kind as possible about it.

It was her virtue that made him look into his own soul to see if he was he acting as honorably as he should. Her integrity, which she never flaunted or even talked about for that matter, made him want to be better, to act better, and to be a nobler human being.

Tony stood up and walked over to the window. Maybe it was unfair to judge Julietta after just a couple of weeks, but he had not found such honor in her. Maybe he had not seen it yet, or maybe he would have to see how she acted under pressure, as he had seen with Amy.

Yes, Amy was a gem, a precious diamond among rocks. "Okay, Tony, so if she's so great, why hasn't she written?" he said out loud. He was furious. "Why hasn't she written? Dammit! Why hasn't she written?"

Sitting down in the chair again, he stared at the letter on the desk for a long time, then he slid it into the envelope, sealing his fate.

* * * * *

"Did you think about it?" Tony asked, placing his napkin on the table.

Looking radiant, Julietta could not contain her exuberance. "Oh Tony, our first time! I love you so! I was at Emily's all afternoon, getting the place ready."

Leaving the diner, they strolled amidst the dimming lights of the city. Tony had his arm around Julietta's waist, and she kept stopping to caress his face and kiss his lips. As they neared Emily's apartment, Tony's spied a cat out of the corner of his eye, and called out, "Tubby!"

Meowing, the cat sauntered over and brushed up against Tony's pant legs. Tony lifted him and scratched his head. "What are you doing here? We need to get you back to the base."

"He's a tomcat. He'll find his way," Julietta said.

"No, I'll take him. I'll meet you at Emily's."

A bit of annoyance flashed from Julietta's eyes. "But Tony, it's our first time! I want to spend every moment with you!"

He walked backward a few steps with Tubby in his arms. "You will! It's just ten minutes. I promise. I'll run."

But Julietta crossed her arms and pouted. "Don't you dare! Don't make me wait. Not now!"

He paused, staring at her and scratching Tubby between the ears. Eventually, he let out a small, sad laugh.

Julietta's annoyance grew from a warm pink to a glowing red. "What's so funny?"

"A stray dog—"

"What?"

"I've got to go," Tony said, walking away.

Juliette shouted. "It's that Jap girl, isn't it? You want her!"

Tony turned around and looked at her. A street light illuminated her hard jaw and intense eyes. He waited a moment before answering her, making sure this was the right thing to do. "Yes, as a matter of fact, I do," he said.

Narrowing her eyes, Julietta stormed toward him. "You're better than that. Us two, we're old country. It's in our veins." She grabbed his arm. "C'mon! We belong together. She could never make you happy, Tony. But me, I understand you."

Tony jerked his arm free. "That's what you don't understand. Amy's special. I didn't understand it myself until last night."

"Dammit, Tony. You've fought the Japs. They killed your best friend. They're savages. And all the Jap women here are prostitutes. Do you really want a Jap whore?"

Clenching his fists, Tony's old anger returned, seemingly out of nowhere. "Don't you ever—" Tubby purred and rubbed her face against his shirt. The vibrations had a calming influence on him. He took a deep breath and stepped back.

"Get real, Tony. She never writes because she's a whore. Is that what you want for your children, a slanted-eyed Jap whore?"

He could not believe what he was hearing. But he was glad for it. How much longer would he have wasted his time with Julietta before seeing this bitterness inside her?

"I've got to go," Tony said, and he left. Her yells of anger followed him until he was out of earshot.

Returning to the barracks with Tubby, Tony sat down at his desk and took out a sheet of paper. Needing to get this out, he lit a cigarette and started writing. *"Amy, I am sorry I have not written in a while. I was confused and hurt. I have not heard from you in so long. After our first date, I prayed for God to make me into the man who could win your heart, and I did that for years. But somehow I got off track. I dated someone else. Please forgive me. I just want to spend the rest of my life with you. I love you."*

Chapter 26

Amy barged into the hospital, searching frantically for her mother. At last she found her tending to an elderly woman. "Mom, is Mr. Fukuoka here?"

"No, what's wrong?" her mother asked, reading the lady's blood pressure.

"Mrs. Fukuoka can't find him." She was out of breath.

"He drinks and wanders around." Her mother sighed. "He could be anywhere."

"But she's worried about him!"

"He's probably passed out somewhere," Mrs. Kashiwagi said, ignoring her daughter and getting back to work.

"Could he be here?" Amy asked.

Her mother scoffed and turned to her patient. "Excuse me one minute, Mrs. Ichiro. I need to help my daughter." She walked past Amy. "I'll check the log."

At the nurse's station, she scanned the clipboard of registered patients. "Nothing here. Come with me." It was a short trip to the hospital morgue. They entered the room and her mother checked the log. The last entry was—*DOA, 2:02 a.m. Person unknown.*

On a gurney, a body was covered with a dirty white sheet. Mrs. Kashiwagi lifted it, and there was the drunken face of Mr. Fukuoka, his eyes closed and a smile on his face. Amy turned away and bit her lip to hold back the tears. Her mother replaced the sheet with a new one. "Maybe it's for best," she said. "He's at peace. He no longer has to live here."

* * * * *

That night, Amy sat with Hiroto outside his family's cell. A ruddy crescent moon, like a bloody wound, passed overhead. "I'm sorry about Mr. Fukuoka," Hiroto said. "I can see you're upset by his death."

"We had become friends," Amy lamented. "Before all of this, he was a respected businessman. I guess if you lived in San Francisco you knew his name. He gave a lot of money to the Japanese American Citizens League. But you know, he and his wife never complained about being here. Now it pains me to see Mrs. Fukuoka so upset. I suppose this place just got to him. It's a shame he had to die here. He should've been at home."

Amy stared down at her dusty shoes. At first, she had believed this place would be temporary, but now she doubted if her feet would ever touch green grass again.

Hiroto squeezed her hand. "I'm glad I met you here."

Amy smiled at him. "I wonder if we will ever get out of here." Uninvited tears rose in her eyes. She dabbed at them with her sleeve. "Has there ever been a war like this one? Perhaps this one will last forever."

"Maybe Japan will win," Hiroto said. "They would take over California, and they would free us."

Amy shook her head. "We left Japan. They wouldn't trust us. They would look at us with as much suspicion as the Americans do. We are between two worlds but part of neither one." Amy dropped her face into her hands.

Hiroto placed his arm around her shoulder. "It's not hopeless. One day, things will be different."

Amy longed for her old apartment, her bed, and her old friends. Other than Hiroto, there was nothing for her here. She looked up at the moon, which seemed to smile a wicked, red smile. Mr. Fukuoka's death had put her in a dark, dark place. It was time to draw herself out. "I spoke to Mr. Tashimergi the other day. I really respect him."

Hiroto nodded. "I think everyone in the camp does."

"A few days ago I asked him if my parents made a mistake in leaving our home country. He said no, that our native land had become militaristic. It was no place for those who sought freedom. He said he had read the American Constitution and, in spite of everything, he still believed in this land."

"Even after everything they have done to us? Hiroto asked.

Amy nodded. "'All nations are flawed, just as all men and all women are flawed,' Mr. Tashimergi said. He believes one day we will be free and we'll take up our lives again and prosper. In the future we will be glad we came to America." Her mood had changed perceptibly. "I don't know why his words touched me so much, but they did. Perhaps one day we will be glad our parents came here."

"Maybe in the distant future," Hiroto murmured.

Amy patted his hand. "Let's change this subject. This is too dreary. Tell me, Hiroto, before this place, did you have a girlfriend?"

The change in subject jarred him. He looked like a batter who had been brushed back with a pitch. The thought made her think of Tony, and she hated herself for it.

Hiroto coughed. "No, not really. I dated a few girls but it was nothing serious. Of course, my parents didn't want me to date any white girls. They want me to marry a Japanese girl."

"Yes, my parents want me to marry a Japanese man. They always objected to Tony." Amy could have bitten her tongue for mentioning Tony.

But Hiroto did not seem unduly disturbed. "Was he your boyfriend before the war?"

She nodded slowly.

"The one you write to?"

"Yes, but he hasn't written back. I guess he has forgotten about me."

"I doubt it. I don't know anything about Tony, but I doubt

anyone could forget you."

"Thank you. That's a very kind thing to say."

"It's also true. Did you love him?"

Amy took her time to answer. She shrugged and smiled a sad little smile. "I thought I did. We dated for a while. We had to sneak around. My parents didn't want him anywhere near the house."

For a long time, they sat in silence; both of them in their own world, with their own thoughts.

Finally, Hiroto spoke into the darkness. "So— will you wait for Tony?" His eyes shone in the moonlight.

"No," she said, though she knew in her heart that she was doing just that, every minute of every day: waiting for Tony.

* * * * *

Tony stood in the murky water, watching his men crossing the small foot path that ran alongside the rice paddy. *Deserts might be a good place to fight,* he daydreamed. *I could get a little sand in my boots, but hey, sand is better than muddy water. I bet there are thousands of germs in the water. Hell, they're more deadly than the Japanese! Or mountains? I should've volunteered to fight the Germans in the mountains of France. At least it is scenic.* His men waited in the dense vegetation as he scrambled across the dirt trail, water squishing in his boots. On this Malaysian island, it was just fields of fetid water, jungles, parasites and leeches, and not much else. *Why do the Japanese want these lousy islands anyway?*

"We have another hour's march before we quit," he said, looking at his troops. "We need to hurry. We don't want the Japs to run away from us, do we?"

"To be honest, Sergeant, I don't think I'd mind that," Private Tim Fullhart said.

Tony still could not get used to being called sergeant. He chuckled, "Neither would I. But I guess we can't give them that option, can we?"

Bivouacking next to a grove of palm trees, Tony took his knife and lopped off the top of a coconut, raising it to his lips and letting the milk drip into his mouth. He leaned against a tree, cutting up the coconut with his knife and devouring the meat. The natural food around the island was far superior to the rations he endured every day.

Corporal Adam Dunn, the medic, came over. Skillfully he unwound the soiled bandage from Tony's neck and dabbed at the wound underneath. "You don't have to be gentle. I expect it's gonna hurt a bit," Tony said, still chewing.

"You're lucky, Sarge. An inch to the left, a half inch to the left, well, for that matter, a quarter inch to the left—"

"And I wouldn't be complaining about bandages."

"No, you wouldn't."

As the medic dabbed the wound with antiseptic, Tony winced. It stung like hell. He remembered the words of a veteran sergeant, who said, "Sometimes when a wound is hurting, you know it's healing."

"You'll be fine by tomorrow," Adam said.

"Are the men okay?"

"Had to pry off a few leeches and deal with some wounds. Abramson got nicked but I bandaged him up. He'll be fine." He tossed the old bandage away and closed his kit. "Do we move out tomorrow?"

Tony nodded. "There's one more hideaway that we have to take from those sons-of-bitches." He leaned back against the tree. His neck ached, his back hurt, and his feet felt like they had walked over a bed of nails. "You know, it's strange."

"What's strange?"

"Back in Los Angeles, I dated a Japanese girl."

"Really?"

Tony nodded. It felt good to talk about Amy, even if she did not love him anymore. "Her parents were rigid, but she was the sweetest girl I'd ever met. She was beautiful, and I mean more than physically attractive. She had the sweetest, gentlest soul, nothing like the Japanese on this island."

The corporal smiled. "I'm from Bakersfield, and I knew a

number of Japanese farmers. True, their homeland attacked us, and we have Jap soldiers right here trying to kill us, but you can't categorize entire races. Every race has a few geniuses and a lot of fools. Hell, I'm Methodist. Our beliefs tell us the entire human race is flawed!" He chuckled and looked out into the night. "Some might be more flawed than others."

"Amy wasn't flawed," Tony said, closing his eyes. He thought about her so long, he did not notice when Adam left.

* * * * *

The bullets from the machine gun kicked up dirt in front of Tony. The Japanese had a superior position on the hill. The platoon fanned out, protected by trees and foliage. Tony's men were on both sides. He waved and pointed toward the pillbox. They understood.

The concrete enclosure was partially hidden. Tony squinted— two men, possibly three. The dense foliage made it impossible to tell. It was best to err on the side of caution—make it three.

The machine gun sputtered again. Bullets echoed around the hill. Tony had not seen any other fire—make it two, the gunner and his feeder. If there was a third Jap, he would be firing too. He looked again, hoping for the impossible. Maybe they would realize their position was untenable and run up a white flag. Fat chance, he thought.

Tony took aim and waited. Sweat beaded on his forehead. Killing the gunner and his loader at this distance was a thousand to one chance, but he could keep them down while his men circled. He fired several times when the gunner came into view, giving his men precious seconds to scramble up the hill. The machine gun turned to the left, spitting out bullets. Tony fired again. The gun barrel dropped and spun around, giving them something to think about.

"Dammit! Not yet!" Tony screamed.

Private Ed Jackson, grenade in hand, charged the machine gun nest. He could not possibly make it. There was too much space between him and the pillbox. But Jackson was faster than Tony thought. The machine gun swung toward him, and he dove into a clump of bushes, throwing the grenade in the same motion. As the bullets zipped over his head, the grenade connected and the machine gun nest exploded in a ball of flame.

As the heat from the blast reached Tony, a bead of sweat rolled down his cheek. He wiped his chin with his sleeve. *Ed, you must have a praying mama.*

Chapter 27

Befitting the image of a respectable, young Japanese lady, Amy sipped her tea with Mr. and Mrs. Yamada. While she disagreed with some of their old-fashioned ways, they were a nice couple.

Mrs. Yamada reached into the cabinet and brought out a thick tome. "Hiroto says you're interested in Japanese culture."

"Yes, I am," Amy said. "Growing up outside the Japanese community in Los Angeles, I really don't know much about Japan. I would like to learn more."

"To understand our culture is to know our language, which is thousands of years old. It's the fabric of our people," Mrs. Yamada said. "This book has been in our family for generations. It teaches our language and customs. Would you be interested in borrowing it?"

"Your offer is so kind," she replied, thinking how rare it would be to learn from such a precious heirloom. "I would like that very much."

Mrs. Yamada smiled and presented the book to Amy, who stood and bowed before she took it from her hands. "This is most gracious. I appreciate this honor very much."

"I hope you will enjoy it."

"I'm sure I will." The more Amy thought about it, the more excited she became to learn about her parents' homeland.

* * * * *

Bullets ripped into the bark of a tree, sending splinters into the air. One caught Tony in the cheek, drawing blood. His temper shot through him, and he raised his rifle and fired randomly. The Japanese were desperate. This was their last outpost—a few shanties protected by barbed wire—on this tropical island. There was no cover outside the compound and no air power available. His squad would have to rush it.

"Dammit! That kid never listens," Tony scowled, spotting Private Michael Perkins trapped in a small ditch, a hundred yards from the Japanese position.

From a prone position Perkins pumped bullets toward the enemy, then cowered as they returned fire.

"Get back here!" Tony yelled. "That's an order!" He signaled his men to pour lead at the enemy, drawing fire from him. He was not sure what Perkins was doing when he ran to the ditch, but whatever his plan was, it was not working. He was completely exposed. Sometimes in battle, men do stupid things. Things they cannot explain. It is a fact of war, usually deadly.

In fear, Michael leaped from the ditch and ran toward his own lines. He stayed low, but a bullet caught him in the thigh. He groaned, hitting the ground. As he tried to stand, a second bullet clipped his shoulder.

"Cover me!" Tony ordered his men. He ran, and guns fired on both sides of him. Bullets dug up dirt all around him. He grabbed Perkins, hoisting him on his shoulder, and ran for his life. Just yards from safety, Tony felt a sudden and fiery pain in his side. He struggled to make the final steps. His left knee touched the dirt, then crumpled to the ground. Perkins was sprawled out next to him. Tony tried to get to his knees, but everything went black.

* * * * *

When Amy was not working, she spent all her free time with Hiroto. He was a nice man, and he got along well with her parents. Mr. and Mrs. Kashiwagi probably thought any Japanese suitor was suitable after Tony. Hiroto played cards with her and her sisters, and even when he lost, he was invariably polite.

The two went to church together, both at the Catholic chapel her family attended and at the Buddhist temple where his family worshipped.

Under the tutelage of Hiroto and Mrs. Fukuoka, Amy took up the challenge of learning Japanese. She would not have taken the time back in Los Angeles, but here, with nothing else to do, she rather enjoyed it. She was impressed by Mrs. Yamada's book, and she soon found herself delving ever deeper into Japanese culture. Also, with a lot of practice, Amy finally learned to eat with chopsticks. She even taught her sisters.

* * * * *

In a hospital robe, Private Perkins hobbled over to Tony's bedside. Weak and ashen-faced, Tony acknowledged him. "Sergeant, thanks for saving my life," Michael said. "That was a helluva risk you took."

"You'd have done the same for me."

"I don't remember much, except you carrying me on your shoulder. I thought we were dead." A tear formed in Michael's eye and slid down his cheek. A second and third joined it. He leaned down and hugged Tony, who realized his face was wet too.

"We're fortunate," Tony said. "We're alive and have all our limbs."

"And there's no gunfire. It's a good day," Michael added with a smile.

"When the war is over, all I'm gonna have are good days," Tony promised himself.

A polite cough came from the doorway. A doctor stood there, tall, thin, and balding on top. "Why, hello there," he said in a deep bass voice. Tony was grateful for the care of Dr. Ben Fitts, an Army veteran. "How's my best patient?" he asked.

"Grouchy, cranky, irritable. I'm ready to get out of here."

Fitts laughed. "Alas, most of my patients are grouchy and cranky. And we treat them so well! You'd wonder why they're so crabby." He smiled at his own joke.

"I'm ready to leave the hospital, doc. No offense to you—you've been great—but I want to get back to the action. My men are out there."

"Understood," Dr. Fitts said, scratching his chin. "You are leaving, but you won't be going back to the action. Not with your wound. You're getting a vacation. The war is over for you. We're sending you home."

Tony's eyes widened in shock "The States?" he spluttered.

"You got another home in mind?" The doctor raised his eyebrows. "You're not fit to go back in combat, Tony. At least not yet. But don't worry. The Army will find something useful for you to do. And remember, do those exercises."

"Congratulations, Sergeant," Michael said, smiling broadly.

"What about you? You were wounded too."

Michael reached into his pocket and brought out his transfer papers. "Look! You'll have company."

Tony stared at the ceiling. This was really happening. A heady mixture of relief, happiness, and guilt coursed through his veins. He hated to abandon his troops, but the images of walking through the kitchen door, kissing his mom on the cheek, and setting out to find the love of his life were simply too irresistible to ignore.

* * * * *

Amy walked along the dusty path for her nightly exercise, wondering for the millionth time if she would ever leave Manzanar. It was a miserable place and perhaps the misery would go on forever. She could not bear such a pointless existence—life and death in a concentration camp.

Deep within her gloom, she walked past Mr. Tashimergi, who was sitting on the steps of his cell.

"Amy, is that you? Why are you so sad this evening?"

She stopped and smiled. Mr. Tashimergi, a popular elder in the camp, always managed to lift her spirits. He was slender, about five-seven, with graying hair and a salt and pepper goatee. It was rumored that he was a martial arts master, but Amy had never asked him if it was true.

She approached him and bowed. "Good evening, Mr. Tashimergi."

"Amy, how are you tonight?"

She shrugged. How was she supposed to answer that question—politely or truthfully?

"Are you troubled, my child?" he asked.

She nodded, trying to hold back the tears, but they spilled, betraying her.

"Sit and tell me what bothers you."

She eased down beside him. "Thank you." The few wrinkles on his kindly face seemed to lend him both dignity and humanity, and there was a discernible sparkle in his eyes.

He opened his hands. "We have all night, and it is a beautiful night."

She nodded, and paused before beginning her story. "Before the war, I dated Tony. He was white and my parents didn't approve. We argued constantly. They want me to marry someone who's Japanese."

He listened with his whole body, and when she was finished, he nodded. "I don't mean to criticize your parents but they are closed in their views. When your parents left Japan, they were moving to a new nation and a new culture. They knew things would be different there. Your parents should have realized their children might fall in love with non-Japanese Americans. They should have prepared for it long before they stepped on these shores."

"I wish they had your wisdom, but they weren't prepared—". Amy tailed off momentarily. "I believe Tony and I had something special. He was polite and funny. He had a very gentle and kind soul."

Listening patiently, Mr. Tashimergi nodded again. "Exceptional traits indeed."

"Yes, but then the war came— I thought we loved each other. I still think of him. I remember his smile and his laugh, the tone of his voice. He told silly jokes. The way he danced. I remember everything about him. I've written him often." She broke into sobs.

"What is the problem, my child?"

"He's never written back!" She looked up, tears overflowing from her eyes. "Not once, Mr. Tashimergi. The worst thing is that I don't know if he's dead or alive! Perhaps he is sick, or captured, or somehow unable to write back? Or maybe he hates me now because of what our country did to his? Maybe he just wants to forget." She wiped a tear from her cheek. "But I know we had something special!" She shook her head. "I'm sorry, Mr. Tashimergi. This is just difficult to explain."

"You are doing a wonderful job, my dear. I can see this Tony clearly in my mind's eye, and I know in my heart what a wonderful fellow he must be to have won your love for him."

"The truth is, well, I can't be sure, but I don't think he's dead. I've checked the war notices in the newspapers every week, and I've never found his name," Amy said, bracing herself for revealing her deepest concern. "So he must have found somebody else. He did have a girlfriend before me. He might have gone back to her."

"It's possible."

"I can't think of any other explanation, except that he's hurt, and I just can't bear to believe that. Oh, Mr. Tashimergi, it's such a mess. I just don't know what to think."

"In life not everything is as it seems," the older man replied. "In times of war, that is especially true. Remember when you have mentioned that you had trouble with a post office clerk?"

"Yes, Corporal Nagy. He— he's the guy who wanted to have his filthy way with me, and when he attacked me, I stuck him with a stickpin."

Mr. Tashimergi peered at Amy in the moonlight. "No doubt he

was very angry. Such a criminal would want to seek revenge on you. What better revenge than discarding your mail, hmmm?" He tilted his head.

Of course! It was as if Amy had been hit by an electrical shock, and hope sprang into her heart. She looked deep into Mr. Tashimergi's eyes. There was nothing but truth there—cold, hard truth. "Yes, that corporal could've done that, and he certainly had the opportunity."

"That is a possibility," Mr. Tashimergi said, scratching his goatee. "I cannot tell you that this is what occurred. In wars, the unexpected becomes the expected. The unpredictable becomes routine."

Amy nodded slowly. "I must have handed him sixty letters. It never occurred to me that he would throw them away."

"That's because your heart is pure. It is not something you would do, or I would do. But often we must consider what other people will do, and we must be aware that they will do things differently than we would. It is the nature of life."

"But Nagy is gone now. I sent a letter after the new corporal came, who would never do something like that, and I still haven't received a reply."

"Amy, you must remember there might be an unforeseeable reason why he can't write."

She sighed. "But it's terrible not knowing anything at all. There is another matter too. I am seeing someone else—Hiroto Yamada—and he's a good man. My parents like him, and he's thinking of volunteering for the war."

"That's very noble." Mr. Tashimergi nodded. "I know him and his parents well."

"Well, I like Hiroto. We have fun and I see no flaw in him. And he likes me too. I'm sure he more than likes me. In fact, he told me he loves me."

"So you are not sure how to react, because there is another man in your heart?"

She nodded. "There is no reason not to date Hiroto if Tony has left me or forgotten me. But what if he hasn't? I have no way of knowing. I just don't know what to do."

Mr. Tashimergi thought for a moment. "You are a lovely girl, but there is a sadness in you. I can see it here." He touched his chest over his heart. "And I can see it in your eyes. Whichever man you choose, I am sure that he will take that sadness and turn it to joy."

Amy shook her head, and her voice became timid. "Can you tell me what to do?"

"My child, I'm afraid that is something I cannot do. That is a decision only you can make after careful thought and meditation—or prayer, if you like. No one should make that decision for you; not I, not your parents, nor anyone else."

"What would you tell your daughter if she had this problem?"

"The same thing I am telling you now. The answer must come from within."

There was silence. A single tear escaped Amy's eye and rolled slowly down her cheek, pausing momentarily, before it splashed onto the dirt below. "Mr. Tashimergi, I believe the answer has already come to me. I have to let Tony go. I have been living in the past too long. I pray that Tony is alive and that he has an abundant life, but I need to start my new life with Hiroto."

"You say he is a good man."

"Yes, he's a very good man." She reached over and touched his shoulder. "Thank you for listening, Mr. Tashimergi. I needed to talk to someone. My parents don't listen. They don't want to hear anything about Tony. I appreciate your guidance."

They both stood up and bowed.

The dull golden glare from the camp light shone on the dark winter coat, sent to her so long ago by her first love. As she walked home, Amy released Tony from her heart and soul. Hiroto was everything she needed in a man, and he was right there in front of her. She realized that the longings she felt for Tony were nothing more than the remnants of a first, sweet love. She would treasure those first dear experiences until her dying days, but now her love belonged to Hiroto.

Chapter 28

"Hello, what can I do for you?" Corporal Lockhart asked, as Mr. Kashiwagi entered the post office.

"Is there any mail for the Kashiwagis?" Amy's father did not know if this soldier was any more trustworthy that the last one to work here, but at least, he did not seem to be stealing from them.

"Let me check."

The corporal left his desk and was back within the minute with two letters in his hand. "You must be Amy's father. Her letter finally got here after all these months."

He nodded. *What letter? And why does he know about this?*

Mr. Kashiwagi took the envelopes and examined the return address—*Tony Piccinin, United States Army.* "I'm sure this will make my daughter very happy."

"Tell her I say hi," Corporal Lockhart said. "I haven't seen her in a long time."

"I will."

Outside the post office, Mr. Kashiwagi opened the letter and scanned it: *I am sorry I have not written— After our first date— I just want to spend— I love you.*

My, that boy was persistent. Even though Tony had sent him his letter jacket when he needed a winter coat, and had helped him move off Terminal Island when he needed assistance, the truth remained—he was still white, still a wop, and it would never work—people need to marry their own *kind.*

Mr. Kashiwagi looked around and dropped the letter in a trash barrel.

* * * * *

Clutching their winter coats, Amy and Mrs. Kashiwagi headed back to their hovel. The temperature was in the high thirties, but the winds whipped off the mountains, slicing through them like sheets of ice. "Mom, Hiroto and I are making plans, before he ships out."

Her mother's smile was warm. "I'm so happy for you. The Yamadas are wonderful people."

"Mom, what do you know about *yui-no*, the engagement ceremony?"

"Oh, honey, everything! You'll need a kimono." Suddenly, her mother's face came alive in a way Amy had not seen in years. It seemed the wheels in her head were spinning faster than she could speak. "Mrs. Sato can make it. The food will be Japanese. Everything will be perfect!"

Entering their cell, her mother went on and on about the perfect Japanese wedding while Amy thought privately of her wedding night. She could not wait for Hiroto to take her in her arms, hold her, kiss her, and remove her clothing in his kind and gentle way. While she and Hiroto had experimented with their clothes on, which was exhilarating, she was now ready to make love for the first time—to become a woman—a wife.

While Amy sat down with Mrs. Yamada's book to reread the chapter on Japanese weddings and plan her own special day, Mrs. Kashiwagi turned her plaid coat inside out.

"What are you doing?" Amy asked.

"There's something in here that keeps poking me." Her mother felt the upper part of the sleeve. "Please, bring me my sewing kit."

Amy went over to the cupboard and pulled out the sewing box. She took it to her mother, and went back to her chair. Once again, she picked up Mrs. Yamada's book and read, as her mother cut the stitching. Her mother reached into the lining of the jacket, and pulled something out that Amy could not quite see.

"Are you okay?" Amy asked, staring at her mom. "You look pale."

"Yes, I'm fine. I have a slight headache."

"What was it?" Amy asked.

"What?" her mother asked, looking flustered.

"What was poking you?"

"Oh, *that*. It was just a piece of straw."

* * * * *

Amy and Hiroto's wedding was the first of three successive marriages for Father Donlon, a Catholic priest. Each ceremony was scheduled for no longer than fifteen minutes. Afterwards, the all newlyweds would share a wedding cake and reception, a disappointment for Amy who had always dreamed of a wedding all to herself. Later that day, Amy and Hiroto would go to the Buddhist temple for a private blessing.

Japanese hand fans and lanterns turned the drab and colorless mess hall into a place of happiness and celebration. The Kashiwagis and Yamadas, excited about the marriage of their daughter and son, buzzed around talking and laughing, greeting and bowing. The tables were covered with yellow and red tablecloths, thanks to a church in Lone Pine. The three-tiered wedding cake was covered in white butter cream with Swiss dots and scroll piping on the corners.

Hiroto, in a United States Army uniform with the patch of the 442nd Infantry Regiment on the shoulder, stood with Father Donlon at the head of the room, as Mrs. Kudo, who had been a pianist with the San Francisco symphony, played the 'Wedding March' in a smooth, melodic fashion on an old upright piano. Wearing a traditional white Japanese wedding kimono with red embroidery, Amy moved slowly down the aisle, as family and friends stood watching her. She took her place beside Hiroto, giving him a shy smile that he returned as though he had just won himself the greatest prize in Manzanar.

Father Donlon, in his vestments, opened his hands in a gesture of welcome and said, "We gather here today for a ceremony of love. These are grim and dangerous times. We only need to look at the newspaper or listen to the radio and hear the chaos and evil in the world. But even in the midst of sorrow, there can be joy. We come here today to participate in the joyous sacrament of marriage, surely the most joyous day in the lives of two young people. In the midst of hopelessness, Hiroto and Amy have found hope. In the midst of gloom, they have found joy and laughter. We are deeply thankful that all of you are here today to share their joy."

For the vows, Father Donlon switched to Japanese, a surprise to everyone but Amy. She wanted the vows to be made in Japanese, and the priest knew enough of the language to officiate. Amy took long, deep breaths to stay calm during Hiroto's vows. Now it was her turn. This was the moment that would define the rest of her life.

"I, Amy," she said in a firm and proud voice. "Take you, Hiroto, for my lawful husband, to have and to hold, from this day forward, for better, for worse, for richer, for poorer, in sickness and in health, until death do us part." There. She had done it. There was a quiet sense of contentment throughout the mess hall.

Father Donlon pronounced the final blessing. "By the authority vested in me by the state of California, I now pronounce you man and wife. What God has brought together, let no man divide. May God bless this union. You may kiss the bride."

She was now Mrs. Hiroto Yamada! She and her husband had made a commitment to love each other from this day forward. Tony was but a distant memory.

Hiroto took Amy's face into his hands and kissed her on the lips. It was the first of many kisses she would receive from him that day.

After the other two services, the photographer took pictures of all three wedding parties and their families. When Hiroto cut a small piece of wedding cake and fed it to Amy, he snapped a photograph, blasting a flashbulb in front of them. A photograph would later show her with icing on her lips.

When all the food was eaten, the photographer raised his hand, requesting everyone's attention. "Will all the men volunteering for the war line up right here." Stepping forward, the three grooms and seven other men looked manly and impressive in their uniforms. Another flashbulb went off.

Amy had never been prouder of her people.

Chapter 29

In a crisp uniform, Sergeant Tony Piccinin watched as the new recruits lined up in front of Master Sergeant Rick Ballast, who stood erect, hands behind his back, chest out, with a disdainful stare on his face. He surveyed the men. They looked so green. One or two of them looked no older than fourteen.

If Tony glanced in a mirror, he guessed he would not look much older than when he walked onto the grounds of Fort Benning. His face was still the same, thinner perhaps, but he felt older. His youthful ignorance and optimism had long disappeared. Rather than a cynical look, his eyes held a weary but wise gaze. At least that was what he hoped.

In the second line he spied Marco, who had written that he would be in the next batch of recruits. Tony was flooded with emotions. He was proud of his little brother, ready to fight for his country, but he had lost his best friend on New Guinea. He had an urge to tell Marco to stay home. There was only blood, death, and horror out there, nothing of valor. But all he could do was leave him to Sergeant Ballast, who would train him well. He prayed that his mother would never have to hang a gold star in the window.

"You think you can become soldiers?" Sergeant Ballast bellowed at the recruits. "You're gonna be fighting the toughest, most ruthless, suicidal bunch of sons of bitches on the face of this earth. The Japs would rather kill you than look at you. Chances are you will want to run back home to your mother. It takes a man to make it through my training. And I'm not sure any of you have the guts for it. Right now we'll give you your uniforms. The question of whether you deserve them or not is still open. Now strip!"

As the recruits fumbled with their clothes, a private walked up to Tony and saluted. "Sergeant, your pass came through."

"Thank you, Private." Tony took the paper and walked over to Ballast. "Master Sergeant, do you see the kid that's built like a ballplayer—the third one in the second row?"

"Yes?"

"He's my brother. Just making a note of it. I'm not asking for any special treatment."

"He won't get any."

Tony nodded. "Good."

"But I will tell him he has a reputation to live up to."

* * * * *

From Fort Hunter Liggett, Tony had hitched several rides to get to his parents' home. He stood on the street, holding his duffle bag, taking in the familiar sights. Everything, the house, the neighborhood looked the same, just smaller. There were three blue stars in the front window for his brother-in-law, his brother, and him. The garage door was up; grandpa's pick-up truck, which Tony inherited, was inside. The family car was gone. He walked up the driveway, remembering himself careening up to the garage on his first bicycle. Opening the kitchen door, he called out, "Mom, Dad!"

Angela, due any day now, appeared from the hallway. Her whole face lit up when she saw him. "Tonyyyy!"

"Hey, sis." Though she looked every bit of a beautiful woman, her eyes were still those of a hopeful child. She opened her arms to him and he put down his bag and fell into them. It felt good to hug her, even with her huge belly in the middle.

"Why didn't you let us know you were coming?"

"I want to surprise everyone."

"But Marco's in—"

"I know. I just left him." Tony smiled.

She stepped back, giving him an admiring once-over. "You're so handsome, Tony. You look the same, but different. Better."

"Wiser?" Tony asked, holding his hat in the crook of his arm.

"No. Not that," Angela said, shaking her head.

Tony laughed. He looked down and tapped her belly. "When's the baby due?"

"Not soon enough," she grumped. "I don't know how Mom did it four times."

"That bad?"

"Yeah, the baby feels like he's marching. Sometimes I feel like I'm in my own war."

He wondered how carrying a life could possibly be compared to the death and destruction he had witnessed, and then he remembered that she had never been exposed to that hell and, thankfully, never would be.

"How's Bruno?" he asked, pulling out a chair for her. He sat next to her.

"Well, thank God. Hopefully, he will be home soon. He says Germany is a wreck."

"I'm glad he made it," he said. The thought of his sister having to raise a child without a father sent shivers down his spine.

"Can I get you something?" she asked, about to get up, but he held her down.

"No, I'm fine. You sit and relax," he said.

"I know war is terrible but we have things to be thankful for," Angela said. "You're home. Bruno is alive. And there's a chance Marco may miss all of the fighting."

Tony looked at his sister. "I'm going to Manzanar. I have to find Amy."

Her reaction was not what Tony expected. He thought she might be angry or upset and tell him to forget about his old girlfriend. But there was nothing angry in her look. She teared up. "What's wrong,

Angela?" he asked, gently.

"I did something awful. You'll hate—" She broke down and sobbed.

"What was it?" Tony asked, putting his hand on Angela's shoulder.

"Please, promise to forgive me?"

"What happened?" Tony asked, wondering if all pregnant women were this emotional.

"I'll be right back." Angela held onto the table, hoisted herself up, and lumbered into her bedroom. She returned a minute later, handing Tony a Japanese stickpin with a distinctive hummingbird design. "I don't know why I took it that night at the dance. Please forgive me. I was such a brat back then."

He stared at the stickpin in his hand, his head filling with memories of Hallowe'en, the dog, the dance, and Amy's composure in the face of it all.

"You know, I was gonna bawl you out that night but she said not to." He rolled the pin over in his hand, remembering all the hours he had spent looking for it. He shook his head. "God, I hope I find her."

"I hope so too." Angela broke into a fresh round of tears.

* * * * *

Kneeling behind the wall, Hiroto heard the rattle of German bullets falling like rain from the church tower in Biffontaine. His squad led the assault, fighting street-by-street, house-to-house, as they died on the cobblestones in this blood-stained town in France. In their last stand, the Germans had taken refuge in the church in front of him, firing from the steeple and the windows with machine guns and rifles, holding the American forces—an all Japanese battalion, the 442nd Infantry Regiment—at bay.

Hiroto turned to Private Ito Hayakawa, a slender and tough fighter at his side. "How do we get ourselves in these positions?"

Ito peered over the wall. "Obviously we picked the wrong tour. I thought I was signing up for the wine country."

"Boy, did you get screwed."

"Yeah, but they gave me ten percent off."

"You still got screwed."

"Tell me about it."

As a bullet pinged off the wall, Hiroto cast a quick glance toward the steeple. The Germans had laid sandbags in the tower as cover. The machine guns roared from just over the top bag. "I'm no general, but I don't see an easy way out of this. Our only option is a direct assault," Hiroto said.

"Shucks, I thought we might wait and starve them out."

"The Army doesn't like to wait," Hiroto said.

Ito looked around as the men got into position. "We're almost ready. They're surrounded."

Their sergeant, situated about twenty yards west of them, ran toward the church. The squad followed with their guns firing. A dozen men to the east of Hiroto sped toward the church. The German gunner turned in their direction and fired.

Hiroto, a crack shot, dropped to one knee to steady himself and fired back. A bullet split the gunner's throat. He aimed again, finding the German sniper in the steeple in his sites. He fired twice. The German plummeted, hitting the ground just in front of the church with a thud.

From a church window, a German raised his rifle and fired at Hiroto.

Instead of taking cover, Hiroto aimed at the second machine gun nest. The gunner's head was a half-inch over the sandbags, a quarter inch too much. Hiroto fired, and when the bullet entered his skull, the German tumbled forward across his machine gun. Two soldiers grabbed his lifeless body and tried tossing him to the side, but the machine gun had trapped one of his arms. By the time the German soldiers pulled his arm free, American forces had climbed through the empty church windows.

Hiroto tried to rise to his feet, but his legs wobbled as he tried to support his weight. He looked down, spotting the two blobs of dark red blood on his torso. He took one step, groaned at the intense pain, and stumbled to the ground. Rolling over, he stared up into the bright sun.

Ito appeared at his side. "They're coming! Help is coming!" But his voice sounded far away as if it were coming through a tunnel.

Hiroto closed his eyes and heard the sounds of Amy's voice in their marital bed, the quiet laughter of his mother during afternoon tea with her beloved friends. All around, the walls of his peripheral vision faded to darkness, and ahead of him was the sun—brilliant, warm, and inviting.

* * * * *

It was the first dinner with his family in over three years, but Tony felt as if he had never left home. His mother served chicken cacciatore, and his father smiled and nodded at everything Caterina told him.

They all wanted to hear about his adventures fighting the Japanese. Knowing they were curious, he provided some details and told some funny stories, then added, "I'd rather not talk about it anymore. There are a lot of things you don't want to hear." The Piccinins took in his words and lowered their heads. They understood and were grateful to have him home.

The rest of the conversation revolved around more routine matters—the new accounts his father had managed to secure, the lasagna his mother made the other day that Grandpa would have loved, and the baby names Angela was considering.

At last, Tony mentioned that he was going to Manzanar to find Amy. Something about the war had brought out the immediacy in him; a need to express anything he was thinking or feeling out of fear that he might not be around another minute to say it. He had spent enough time holding in his feelings for Amy before the war, but now there was nothing they could do about it. He was a man, not a child, and if they had a problem with it, they could take it up with him.

A deathly silence fell upon the dinner table.

"I hope you find—" Angela said, before her mother cut her off with a cold stare.

"I don't get it," his mother said. "She never wrote to you, and here you are still hankering for her!"

"Maria!" Antonio eyed her.

But his mother continued, "The Japs had it easy. Everything was provided for them. There was no hardship or rationing in those relocation camps, and you got shot up. They are the ones who started this, bombing Pearl Harbor. Besides, you know, she's married by now."

"Maria, don't make an opera out—" his father said.

"Dad," Tony said, shooting out a hand. "It's okay. She probably is. I don't know what I'm gonna say. I just want to be sure she's okay. That's all."

After a long, painful stare, his mother nodded, her first sign of understanding in years.

"What about Julietta?" she asked.

"She wrote me. She's moving back to San Diego with her mom."

"I'd like to meet her," his mother said.

"It's not gonna happen, Mom," Tony said, his eyes level with hers. "It's over between us. Just accept it."

Chapter 30

Setting off for Manzanar, Tony left Grandpa's pick-up truck at home in case it was needed to transport Angela to the hospital. The weather was sunny but not too hot—a good day for hitchhiking in the desert. In his sergeant's uniform, Tony cocked his thumb out. It would not be long before he got a ride. Everyone was eager to give a soldier a lift.

It had taken three rides and six hours for Tony to reach Lone Pine. He stood before a road sign: *Independence 16*, and flashed his charming Italian smile. He was only eight miles from Manzanar. A dirty, rattling pick-up truck rumbled onto the side of the road. The driver, a burly man with sun-burned skin, craned his neck out the window and said, "Get in, soldier."

"Thanks." Tony slid in, and the driver hit the gas pedal. Country music played on the radio. Tony had never cared for it much, but now it tickled his ears. He tapped the window-sill to the bluegrass beat.

"Got a cigarette?" the driver asked.

Tony pulled a pack from his shirt pocket, giving him one.

"Thanks. I haven't had a chance to stop. You fight overseas?"

"Yeah, I did some island hopping in the Pacific, until a few bullets caught me. They sent me to Fort Liggett to be an instructor."

The driver nodded, waiting for him to expand his answer, but when he did not, he just looked toward the highway. Tony figured he was not the first soldier he had picked up who did not want to jabber on about war stories.

Tony grinned when he recognized the song on the radio, 'Shame on You' by Spade Cooley. In a twangy voice, the singer called out his unfaithful girlfriend, doubting she was losing any sleep over him. Tony wondered if that was the case with Amy as he mouthed the words to the chorus.

When the song ended, the radio announcer broke in. "We interrupt this program to bring you this breaking news. Just an hour ago, Emperor Hirohito of Japan announced Japan's surrender. President Truman will address the nation at three o'clock. Stay tuned for additional updates."

The driver banged on the steering wheel and exclaimed, "Did you hear that? It's over! The war is over!"

Tony felt as if the world had stopped moving. He could not speak. It was over. He could go home, find a job, meet a good girl, and get married.

"It's the atomic bombs, that's what done it," the burly guy said. "We showed 'em who's boss." He took a drag on his cigarette. "Damn Japs! We should dump a few more on them and make them pay. That's what I says."

Tony felt the old familiar red anger return, but it was easier to simmer down nowadays. People were entitled to their own opinions.

"Where you headed, soldier?"

"Manzanar."

"What are you doing at the Jap camp?"

"I'm visiting an old girlfriend."

"She works there?"

"No, she's a prisoner."

"A Jap?"

Tony turned to him. How could he make people understand? Just as there were Americans who were Italian and Americans who were redneck like the driver, there were Americans who were Japanese as well. He tried to make his voice friendly but firm. "Sir, I fought the Japanese. She's an American of Japanese descent," he clarified. "She was born in this nation and she is a citizen. She's a sweet and gentle woman."

"Don't make no difference. A Jap is a Jap."

Tony's glare turned into Arctic ice. "Stop the truck."

"Ain't no good to get riled up. I can drop you off—"

"I'll get out here."

The driver looked at him, but Tony's hard scowl was too much for him, and he shifted uncomfortably in his seat, gazing back at the highway. "Suit yourself." He slowed the truck and eased it onto the shoulder of the highway. He looked up toward the sun. "It's at least five miles. You'll bake."

"Is that all?" Tony said, as if he had not walked longer than that with a Garand rifle strapped to his back in enemy territory.

A minute later, another driver picked him up, an attorney headed to the county courthouse in Independence. When asked where he was going, Tony grunted, "Manzanar." He did not add any details, and the driver did not ask. He just nodded and drove on in complete and beautiful silence.

The lawyer dropped him off at the front gates where two lackadaisical guards stood. "I'm here to visit a prisoner," Tony said.

"Yes, Sergeant. All visitors need to check in at the Commander's office."

"That's fine. Where is it?"

"I can show you the way."

Tony followed him. The soldier opened the door to headquarters, then escorted him into a large, opulent office. A muscled officer with not an ounce of fat on him looked up from the desk. They saluted, and the general returned the salute.

"Sir, Sergeant Tony Piccinin, he's here to visit someone."

"Thank you, Private. That's all." He offered his hand, and Tony appreciated the firm shake. "General Ted Forrest. Good to meet you, Sergeant."

"Thank you, sir."

"Please sit down, Sergeant. What can I do for you?"

"Sir, I'd like to see a friend of mine," Tony said, lowering himself into the most uncomfortable chair he had ever encountered

"He's stationed here?"

"No, she's a prisoner. She was my girlfriend, sir."

"Oh." It was only a one-syllable word but there was a lot of judgment packed into the two letters. Forrest's stern expression did not change but everything else did. "What's her name, Sergeant?"

"Amy Kashiwagi, sir."

He nodded. "Sergeant, I know the Kashywaguy family. I can tell you how to get to her residence."

"Thank you, sir."

He waited, as the general stood, moved to the window, and gave him all the details, right turns, and left turns. Once he had all the information, Tony thanked him and turned to leave.

"I'm sorry, Sergeant," the general said.

"So am I, sir," Tony replied, shutting his door.

As Tony made his way through the concentration camp, he noticed how the Japanese men and women, old and young, looked defeated and demoralized. They knew the war was over, but still they ambled with their heads down, shoulders slumped. Even the few Japanese who surrendered in the Pacific had not looked this bad. As Tony passed by, the prisoners crossed to the opposite side of the path to avoid him. Maybe his uniform scared them, or perhaps, after years behind barbed wire, it was the effect of all white Americans.

Tony turned left when he reached the block where the Kashiwagis lived. His heart froze when he recognized the beautiful young woman on the front step holding a swaddled baby in her slender arms.

"Amy."

She stared at him as though she had seen a ghost. "Tony?"

It had been forty-two months since that day in Malibu—three and a half of the longest years he had ever lived.

Her eyes were glued to him. "Tony?" she repeated

"Amy, I've been worried sick over you."

"You're alive? You're okay?" Amy asked, standing up, her

knees shaking.

"Yeah, I'm okay." He tried to smile, but the endless years of hardship, blood and death on foreign islands, and of watching friends die, came between them like the plundering waves of an ocean. "How are you?" he asked.

"What are you doing here?

"I came to see you. You look the same." Tony looked down at the child. "Is this your baby?

"I had a boy—Hiroto," she said, still in shock. "He's named after his father."

A lump came to his throat, but he gulped it back down. She had not waited for him, which was fine. She was married, just like his mother said. At least he knew she was all right.

"He has some of your features," Tony said, stealing glances at the baby, until he noticed a gold star in the window. Amy followed his gaze. His throat went dry. "Your husband?"

"He died in Biffontaine, a little town in France."

"I'm sorry." He could not believe that her husband was dead. All of his problems now seemed so trivial. He felt selfish and unworthy. *God, please forgive me!*

"He was very courageous," Amy said.

Tony nodded, as tears came to his eyes. "How are you holding up?"

"It's hard. I loved him so much. He was everything—" Amy started to choke up. "But I have to move forward. I have Hiroto. Loss, I guess, is a part of life. You'd have liked him, Tony."

God, this was the same old Amy. Her husband was dead, and she said he would have liked him. She was right. He would have respected anyone married to her.

The door opened, and Mr. Kashiwagi walked out. Tony hardly recognized him. He was stooped, shoulders rounded, hair gone white. When he walked, he shuffled his feet, like a man in his seventies, but he could not have been more than fifty or fifty-two. Deep lines crisscrossed his face, and disappointment dulled his eyes.

"Dad, you remember Tony?"

Mr. Kashiwagi peered at him. "Ah, the conquering hero has come back to claim his spoils." He bent his head and spat at Amy's feet. "You should be ashamed of yourself! You have a child to think of."

Tony stepped forward, and Amy moved to restrain him. But there was no need to. "Mr. Kashiwagi, the war was hard on everyone. But it's over now. I have always respected you and your family," Tony said, holding out his hand. "Can we figure out a way to live together?"

"Never!" Mr. Kashiwagi said, sneering at him and spitting on his boots.

"Dad!" Amy exclaimed, but Mr. Kashiwagi shuffled away.

Amy turned to Tony. "Would you like to hold him?"

"Can I?" Tony was honored. He had not held a baby since Caterina was born.

She handed him the plump infant.

"Like this?" he asked, holding him in the crook of his arm.

"Yes. Keep his head elevated."

There was a strange silence between them, but the remnants of their old friendship remained, just under the surface.

"So, how about you? Are you married?" Amy asked.

Tony looked up from the baby. "I was serious with a girl on Hawaii, but we never married."

She nodded in understanding, but what more she might be thinking, he did not know. "It's good to see you again, Tony. I've often thought about you. But why are you here?"

"I had to make sure you're okay. I have something for you." He reached into his pocket and brought out a small case, handing it to her.

Amy opened the case carefully. She gasped, "My grandmother's stickpin!"

Then suddenly, Amy looked from the pin to Tony, and her eyes welled up with tears. Tony knew something was terribly wrong. Her voice rose. "Two years I wrote! And nothing! Not a word! And now you show up with this?"

"What?" he asked, trying not to startle the baby. "I wrote! I wrote every week, Amy! I never got a reply."

"I never received them!" Amy wiped her eyes with her sleeve.

"I— I don't understand," Tony said. "Amy, I thought about you constantly. Many times, the thought of you was what kept me going in a tough situation. I never received a reply."

Her eyes widened. There was both sadness and recognition in her face. "I think I know what happened." She shook her head.

"Tell me."

As Tony held Hiroto, Amy told him about Corporal Nagy and how he tried to rape her, about the stealing, and the eventual transfer of Nagy and the others. Amy added, "I talked about you to a very wise man here. He has since passed away. But he suggested the clerk might have destroyed my letters. I now suspect that's what happened. Nagy was angry with me. He probably threw away all of your letters addressed to me too."

"Damn him to hell!" Tony cried, bristling with anger and forgetting to keep his voice calm for the baby. "The Army shouldn't have transferred him. They should've shot him!"

"I wrote to you after he was transferred, Tony," Amy said. "What happened to that letter, I don't know."

"Amy, if I ever get my hands on Nagy—"

"None of that matters now." She reached over and squeezed his hand. "As my elderly friend would say, we should not dwell in the past, even if it is not quite past yet."

"He's right," said Tony, the old red mist beginning to clear. "You're okay, and your son is okay. That's all that matters."

The baby laughed and playfully slapped Tony's cheek. "Yes, we can be thankful for that," Amy said, "Except, Hiroto doesn't have a father."

"Don't worry," Tony said, stroking the baby's hair. "He'll grow up with one."

Chapter 31

Tony eased his truck between two white lines in front of the Los Angeles County Building. In his dress blues and slicked back hair, he opened the door for Amy, and she stepped out, holding Hiroto in her arms. "How long will it take to get the license?" she asked.

"Ten to twenty minutes at most," Tony said, helping her onto the sidewalk.

On the courthouse steps, a crowd of about two hundred people, including reporters and photographers, had gathered in front of some microphones. "What's going on?" Amy asked.

"Looks like some type of press conference." Tony spotted a man with his wife, two daughters and a son, in an Army uniform, behind the podium.

The man stepped up to the microphones, and Amy got a clear view of his face, "That's Mr. Schultz!"

A nearby man, wearing a huge red, white and blue *Schultz For Mayor* button on his lapel, overheard her. "You know him?" he asked. When neither Amy nor Tony responded, he added, "He's running for mayor."

Amy and Tony exchanged pointed glances, then watched as Mr. Schultz, in a blue pinstripe suit, bellowed, "Ladies and gentlemen, today I am announcing my candidacy for the office of mayor of this great city. Now that the war is over, the citizens of Los Angeles need and deserve a mayor who can lead it to prosperity, and I am that man!"

Cheers erupted all around.

Tony and Amy moved around the crowd and walked up the courthouse steps. He laughed to himself, shaking his head.

"Is there something funny?" she asked.

He turned and looked at the press conference. "In an odd, bizarre sort of way, it seems appropriate for that crumb to be running for mayor."

"Let's just hope he doesn't get elected."

They entered the courthouse to stares of disbelief over a white man in a military uniform walking with a Japanese woman, but they kept their chins up and strolled past them into the Justice of the Peace office.

After waiting, while others glared at them or murmured poorly disguised comments behind cupped hands, the clerk finally called their number.

"Twenty-two, that's us," Tony said, standing and helping Amy up.

Gesturing for them to sit down in his office, the clerk asked, "May I help you?"

"Yes, we want to get married," Tony said, holding Amy's hand. The clerk did not respond. He only looked at the baby in Amy's lap. Tony continued, "Her husband was killed in the war. We love each other, and I would like to raise the boy as my own."

The clerk shifted uneasily in his seat. "Sergeant, did you fight overseas?"

"Yes, I fought in the Pacific."

The clerk glanced at Amy. "My brother died at Guadalcanal, and I had several friends in the Pacific. I know what you went through. So I say this with regret. I can't give you a marriage license."

"Why not?" Tony leaned forward.

"It's against the law. California doesn't allow mixed-race marriages."

"But that's unfair. There must be a way."

"Sergeant, this has been a California law for quite some time. I wish I could, but I am forbidden to give you a license."

Tony stared at the man in dismay. He seemed genuine enough. "You mean to tell me I fought for my country and now I can't marry the woman I love?"

"Not in this state. Even if I wrote you a license, it would be nullified by state law. As I said, I regret this."

The old familiar temper flared in Tony, but he kept it under control, when all he really wanted was to slam his hand down on the desk and demand that a certificate be written for him. With an even breath, he asked, "Do you know which states allow mixed-race marriages?"

"New Mexico is the closest."

Tony looked over at Amy. Her eyes seemed to reflect her inner torment. "Then we're gonna take a drive," he said to her. "I'm sorry, honey, but we're not gonna make it to Santa Barbara for our honeymoon."

"That's okay. I'd much rather go to New Mexico anyway." She smiled. God, she was beautiful. In the face of every adversity, she never let it get to her. She always kept her composure.

As Tony and Amy stood up to leave, the clerk said, "Sergeant, I wish you the best of luck. You too, ma'am."

"Thank you," Tony said.

"You are very kind," Amy said, rocking Hiroto who was fussing.

Chapter 32

While Hiroto slept in her arms, Amy studied the map. "We're not far from the border, and then twenty miles to Gallup."

"Good," Tony said, looking at his watch. "If we don't have another flat, there should be plenty of time to get the license this afternoon and then we can get married." On their first day out, they had crossed the Colorado River and entered Arizona. For Amy, it was her first time in another state. Every time they stopped for gas, she purchased a postcard or two. On day two, they had enjoyed the scenic drive to Winslow, Arizona.

Amy was silent for a while. She smiled as she admired the contours of the baby's face. "Tony, I want to tell Hiroto about his father."

"Of course," Tony said, nodding at her. "He should know how courageous his father was. We can put his medals in his room."

She reached over and touched his hand. "Thank you. That means so much to me."

They passed a road sign: *New Mexico 35*.

* * * * *

Tony had parked outside the McKinley County Courthouse in Gallup. It was a small, two-story building. Amy had fallen asleep before they arrived, but soon, her eyes opened, as she glanced around. "Are we here?"

"He's ready for his grand entrance." Tony held up Hiroto. He was such a cute little fellow. Tony had never in his wildest dreams expected to ever change a diaper or feed a baby—that was woman stuff—but he had done both, several times, over the last two days.

Amy smiled at Tony, took the baby into her arms, and together, they entered the courthouse. They found the office marked Justice of the Peace and walked in. "Marriage license?" the lady asked.

"Yes," Tony replied.

"You must be from California!" She laughed.

"How did you know?"

The middle-aged clerk, somewhat stout, wore a beaming smile. "You know why. Silly law. Please sit down. I'll need some information."

When she finished typing the marriage license and duplicating it for her files, she handed it to Tony. "It's a bit late today so Judge Allanson has already left, but if you come back at nine tomorrow morning, he can marry you. The judge is also a Presbyterian minister, so it's kind of a double duty for him. We have a florist just down the street," she said, gesturing to the street behind them, "and for a small fee, he can provide a beautiful bouquet for the bride. We always grab two courthouse employees to serve as witnesses. Mrs. Oberson is a romantic and just loves weddings. We also have a local photographer who will snap a few photographs of the handsome groom, the beautiful bride, and the, uh, young gentleman," she said, eyeing the baby.

"Thank you," Amy said, blushing.

Tony ran a hand through his hair. "Wow, that's awfully kind of you. I mean, we weren't expecting—"

"Well, we allow mixed-race marriages so we get couples from several states. It's a little cottage industry here!" She laughed. "Both the photographer and the florist are on call, and because you're a serviceman, you get a twenty-five percent discount."

"Can't argue with that," Tony said.

* * * * *

At nine the next morning, Judge Allanson, also known as Pastor Allanson, stood with Tony in the small room converted into a chapel at the back of the courthouse. There was no music, but neither Tony nor Amy seemed to mind. Amy looked splendid in a pale blue dress, holding a bouquet of red and white carnations assembled by the florist. A carnation held up her hair on one side, over her ear. The photographer snapped a few photos of her as she walked down the makeshift aisle.

Mrs. Oberson did indeed love weddings, and proved to be a most memorable witness. She beamed and held back tears as Amy joined Tony before the judge.

"Every marriage is unique and special," Judge Allanson began. Tony could not wait to hear what he had to say after interviewing them just before the ceremony. "But this marriage that we celebrate today is even more special than usual. Before us are two young people who were separated by war. Before Pearl Harbor, Tony and Amy fell in love. When war came, Tony was drafted and spent several years fighting in the Pacific. Amy, with her family, was sent to a concentration camp in Manzanar, California. We're not here to discuss the wisdom or fallacy of such a policy. But we can note it was terrible that these two young people were separated."

Amy sniffed, doing her best not to cry, and Tony's fingers tightened around her hand. Every so often, Amy looked over at Hiroto, bouncing in Mrs. Oberson's lap.

The judge continued, "Due to circumstances, they were unable to communicate with each other until the war was over. But in the aftermath, they found each other again, and their love for one another, which had never died, sprang forth in all its beauty and splendor. They tried to get married in California." He shrugged, eliciting soft chuckles throughout the room. "But we all know about California's laws."

"Yep," Mrs. Oberson grunted, as happy tears streamed down her face.

"Now, finally, after all the obstacles and troubles that have plagued them, Tony and Amy are here to pledge their love for one another."

There were a number of "ahhs" from the witnesses, who had grown from two to eight since the judge began speaking. When Tony and Amy repeated their vows, they squeezed each other's hands and smiled.

"By the authority vested in me by the state of New Mexico and by my authority as a minister of the gospel, I now pronounce you man and wife. This union of Mr. and Mrs. Antonio Piccinin is officially recognized by the State of New Mexico and we ask the blessings of God the Almighty upon this couple, this child, and all other children that might come from this union. After all you have been through, may joy, peace, and love now surround you this day and forever. You may kiss the bride."

As tears flowed down their faces, Tony pressed his lips upon his wife's. They laughed, foreheads touching. At last, they were married and nothing would ever separate them again.

The End

Epilogue

Sandra beamed at the cake with her sparkling brown eyes, then squealed with delight as Tony lit the three candles. Her oldest brother, Hiroto, sat beside her, and Paul, her five-year-old brother, stood next to her, eyeing the cake as though he wanted to plunge his fingers deep inside it. Dominic, her baby brother, rested in their mother's arms. He would be the last, Amy and Tony had decided. With four children, there was enough laughter and joy in their house to last a lifetime.

Gathering around the little girl, Mr. and Mrs. Kashiwagi and the family sang, "Happy Birthday, dear Sandra, Happy Birthday to you!" She drew a deep breath, made a wish, and blew out the candles. Everyone applauded, and Tony cut the cake.

It had taken a while, but the children's maternal grandparents were here. Tony and Amy could not have been more thrilled. Perhaps the birth of Paul five years earlier had helped. Contact had been tentative and always brief before he came into the world, but when Paul was almost two months old, her mother had called and asked if they could come over and see their grandsons that afternoon.

Amy's answer was yes. She thought the visit would be brief, but fifteen minutes with Hiroto and Paul stretched to thirty minutes and then to an hour. When Mrs. Kashiwagi put the baby down for his nap, she sat by his crib and hummed an old Japanese lullaby. She sat there till Paul fell asleep. With tears streaming down her cheeks, she came out and hugged her daughter, and told her she was sorry it had taken her so long to visit the baby.

Mr. Kashiwagi was a little bit more reticent. He and his wife were leaving that day when Tony drove into the driveway from work. As Amy's father opened his car door, he said to Tony, "They're fine boys."

"Thank you."

"I would like to see them again. If that is okay with you?"

"You're welcome here any time," Tony replied. "This house is your home too."

Mr. Kashiwagi bowed to him, a gesture that rendered Tony speechless. Never did he think he would live to see this day. In a soft voice, her father said, "Please forgive me."

And since that day, Amy's parents had been present at every birthday and holiday.

Sandra shouted with delight for the first piece of birthday cake. She grabbed both cake and icing with her hands and brought the piece up to her mouth. Her mother shook her head, laughing, and said, "It's her birthday. I'm going to let her eat with her hands!"

Tony cut several pieces and passed the plates to everyone. "We're having a lot of birthdays in this family, and I'm getting fat," Amy pretended to complain.

"Being chubby means you have lived a good life. Look at me!" her mother said. She reached over and patted her husband's hand. "Even your father is putting on a little weight. We are blessed."

Sandra licked her fingers, and icing was smeared on her lips and cheek. "Next year, you are going to use a fork," Amy said, wiping her face with a napkin and remembering the photograph from her first wedding, where she had icing on her mouth.

Out of the corner of her eye, Amy saw a blue Ford pull up in the driveway. Her in-laws drove that same model. As everyone chatted, she walked to the living room window with Dominic in her arms. Mr. Piccinin stepped out of the driver's seat, stared at the house for a minute, as though checking to see that they had found the right address, and circled around to the passenger's side door.

Through the screened door, Amy overheard her father-in-law speaking to her mother-in-law. "How long are you gonna hold onto this? It's time to bring the family together. We have grandchildren."

"We have *Japanese* grandchildren," Mrs. Piccinin protested.

"They're Japanese-Italian, and they're *ours*. Amy is a wonderful wife to Tony. How long will it take before you realize that?"

His wife remained silent.

"Come on. It's a party!" Antonio said.

Maria neither nodded nor replied. She just stared straight ahead. "At least give me the present," he said, with frustration in his voice.

She handed him a square box, covered in wrapping paper and tied together with a pink ribbon and bow, and he brought it to the front door. Amy retreated down the hall, but he must have seen her, because he stopped. He stiffened and looked back at the car, as though he was considering whether he should continue. But he rang the doorbell, and Amy opened the screen door with a big smile. "Mr. Piccinin, what a lovely surprise! Won't you please come in?"

"For Sandra," he said, holding out the gift.

"Thank you. I'm sure she'll love it." As Amy took the package, the baby moved into his grandfather's arms, preventing him from saying no.

"Ha!" Amy laughed with a smile that could melt ice. "Dominic likes you. Please come in. We're having cake, and Tony would be thrilled to see you."

"I can only stay a second," he said, looking back at the car.

As Amy led her father-in-law into the back part of the house, she glanced back every so often to see how he was doing with the baby in his arms. The children and the Kashiwagis did not notice him at first, since they were huddled around the table, but Tony did.

"Dad," he said, closing the pantry door.

"Tony. It's been so long."

"I'm so glad to see you," Tony said, coming up to his father and giving him an awkward hug, clearly unsure how much affection his father wanted to handle at the moment. "Dad, you remember Amy's parents, Mr. and Mrs. Kashiwagi?"

"It's been a long time. How are you doing?" Antonio said, shaking hands with Mr. Kashiwagi.

Mr. Piccinin turned toward Amy and said, "May I hold my grandson for another minute?"

"Of course."

"He looks like Tony," his father said, looking at his grandson.

"A little bit, but he has his mother's eyes." Tony said, smiling at Amy, as the baby gurgled and slapped his small hands on his grandfather's cheek. "Is Mom here?"

"She's out in the car."

Tony headed to the front window, followed by his wife, his father, and his sons, and saw his mother sitting in the passenger seat. "Maybe if we went out with Dominic, she might be persuaded to join the party."

"We can try," Amy said.

"I think that's a great idea," Mr. Piccinin said, bouncing the baby in his arms.

As the adults walked outside, Amy motioned for the boys to follow them. Nearing the car, Antonio held up Dominic. "Maria, why don't you come out, so you can see our grandson better? Isn't he handsome? He looks a bit like Tony, don't you think?"

Tony leaned in the window to greet his mother. Her eyes were filled with tears. "Mom, these are your grandsons. Come out and say hi to them. They want to meet you. C'mon."

Mrs. Piccinin blew her nose and dabbed at her eyes. "Oh, fine," she said, her voice wavering. Slowly, her hand reached for the door. She held the handle for a moment, then snapped it open. With Tony's help, she stood up and looked at her newest grandson. Dominic, possibly aware that he was the center of attention, laughed and clapped his hands.

"Did you hear that? He has Tony's laugh," Amy said.

"Why, Amy, I didn't see you there," Maria said, blinking a tear away and holding her hands out. "May I hold him?"

"Sure," Amy said.

Dominic did not seem to mind being passed around. After his mother kissed the baby, she glanced down at Paul and Hiroto.

"Hiroto is my oldest," Tony said, putting an arm around his son. "And this is Paul."

"Yes, my grandsons, my grandsons," Mrs. Piccinin repeated, as though she was convincing herself.

"You must come in and see Sandra," Tony added. "Now she looks like a Sansone!"

"Yes, thank you," his mother said, as Tony ushered her into the house. She touched Paul's shoulder with her free hand. "You're a good looking young man."

Hearing the screen door open, Sandra ran out of the kitchen to see who it could be. She stared up at her grandmother, not knowing who she was.

"Oh, she's beautiful. I see the family resemblance, but really—really she looks just like her mother." Maria said, handing the baby to Amy. "Her lovely mother." She opened her arms to her granddaughter, who looked at her mom for approval. Upon seeing the nod of her mother's head, she ran into her grandmother's arms.

"Sandra, Sandra. Oh, what a lovely child. My granddaughter!" she cried, picking her up.

Amy reached over and touched Maria's dress. "Oops, you got a little icing on you."

"That's all right." She kissed Sandra, who giggled with glee.

Stay connected with the author, your thoughts and comments are welcomed
www.betweentwoworldsthebook.com
If you would like to make a contribution to honor the 120,000 Japanese-Americans who were imprisoned during World War II with a monument on the Nation's Mall, please visit the website.

Manufactured by Amazon.ca
Acheson, AB

12682558R00122